CHIMERO

CHIMERO
SAM FARAHMAND

dD

Chimero
Copyright © Sam Farahmand, 2020

Published by dD
Cover Design by Luke Wiget
Interior Design by Nick Rossi
Cover Photo by Matt Conant
Author Photo by Chris Parsons

ISBN 978-1-950987-02-3

for my mother

THE LOST ONES
PART ONE

The lost ones, Adam said. We're the lost ones, aren't we. The ones who wouldn't have some great war to go to and wouldn't come back knowing what we're supposed to do, no, we're all here now, all alive but not sure where to start living, with no certainty to begin with, because there's no end to everything that came before this. Adam and I stood in between the third and fourth in a row of shedding palm trees, tall and thin with bottom halfs folded over into dried brown dresses, an hour until midnight and still hot, in the wet grass where we went to drink after the sprinklers had gone off on their own and in the time it took to turn them off had emptied everyone else out of the end of the backyard. We're all in our early twenties of this post-post-war generation, but we're all lost, we're all a lost generation, *a* lost generation not *the* lost generation, not *the* but *a*, just sort of here but not at all really, here not there, here but not here, in a city of sorts. We drank and Adam said nothing else about the ones in black and white circling two at a time to the three piece jazz band playing under the stretched white canvas of a string lit canopy before he shook his head and with a hard *g* like angle instead of angel he said, Los Angeles.

Adam looked like a child from having his wisdom teeth pulled earlier that week, but smiling in between smaller and smaller sips he held his cup up to his swollen cheeks, the ice in the drink as much as the drink making him feel good. He had been selling me his painkillers for a few dollars each. He didn't need them.

It's this city that's fake enough to make you want to look for something real, I told him. But at least the superficiality here's only skin deep.

He nodded and he shook the ice in his cup then shrugged and emptied it all into his mouth and motioned that he was going to go back inside. I had neared the end of my drink but stayed where we were and I tilted my head back to drink some and stare at the tops of the palm trees and at the fronds cutting dark shapes out of the night. It was hot and my suit didn't fit right. The others were in their jackets and ties and in evening dresses and I didn't know where else to go.

The bar at the side of the canopy looked lonely once the song started slowing down enough to sound almost like a waltz, enough to attract all the ones who couldn't dance but could stand close to each other and shuffle back and forth, moving the way dancers moved and didn't go anywhere. I headed for the bar and everything there was to do in between drinks, still walking straight if not sober, but my shoes sank me into the wet ground and slowed my steps and made me move in the same sort of three-fourths time as the ones dancing, though I had gotten there after most of them and hadn't danced and didn't want to, looking instead for the ones out of the hundred or so in the backyard who stayed as they were when the songs slowed, the ones who were there to drink and were the same but a little older from the year before. I left muddied footprints the first few steps across the checkered pool cover to what had turned into a self-served mess of a bar for how early it was, unfinished drinks left between all the browns and whites and aperitifs and digestifs out of order on the black tablecloth. There was a mixed drinks menu left from when someone was there to play bartender, in line with each cocktail name the price of $0.00, under that listed what was in them, more for the bartender most likely than for the bartendee, but there were citrus rinds stuck to the laminate and everyone had to be their own for the time being.

There was always someone to kiss at midnight. How many times she had kissed someone else at midnight or someone else from the year before, even me, I couldn't know, but maybe there was someone who hadn't, someone I hadn't met and could talk to without wondering how many times she had kissed someone there.

I finished my watered down drink knowing I would pour from the same brown bottle with the handful of ice that hadn't melted in my glass, maybe take another handful and pour some more.

Look at this fucker. There was a hand on my shoulder and I dropped the ice into my glass and was half turned around to see a thin auburn mustache and eyes opened wide behind horn-rimmed glasses. He was short with combed hair and a blue pinstriped vest that evened him out despite his height and made him seem wide. I heard you were around.

Who'd you hear that from.

Adam.

Right, I said. The brown bottle wasn't as heavy as last time, though the bottles weren't that far from full and even then there would be more to drink inside when most of them left, the word of mouth sort who were always at the parties in the winter when everyone came back for a month. I poured as much scotch as before but it went closer to the top of the cup and I said to him, Pick your poison. He was looking down at a cigarette he seemed to have been struggling to roll before he had come over to talk to me, though he might not have if he hadn't been walking while looking down.

It's all the same isn't it.

I guess it is and it isn't.

I'll have the same then.

I took an empty cup that had been left face up and a handful of ice and poured him the same. I left the bottle with a cheaper whiskey and held up my cup to him and said, Veneer your venom. It tasted better to me than it did before, but the one with horn-rimmed glasses frowned and exhaled after he drank and went back to pinching the tobacco between his thumb and forefinger to stretch it out across the rolling paper. I heard there might be some blow.

Who'd you hear that from, he asked me.

Adam.

That fucker.

The music picked up again while everyone but the one

11

with horn-rimmed glasses watched the band tremble with that up and down movement jazz musicians have out of the sound they make, the dancers slow to circle outward as the same up and down went straight to their feet on its way through their bodies, twisting through each limb, their arms going back and forth as much as up and down until it changed in the end and their heads went back not up and forth not down. They danced as their shadows danced around the edges of the canopy, shortening themselves, standing up straight again, some of them spinning until they dissolved or dizzied themselves and stumbled out somewhere different than where they had first gotten on, before an almost manic lilt between the second and third steps had thrown them off. They were all drunk off of nothing at all.

Are you seeing this, I asked and I drank. I think I've been up and awake for three days now.

The one with horn-rimmed glasses said something that was lost in the crescendo.

There were the ones on the other side of the canopy where the furniture from inside the house had been moved to the patio and left in plastic slipcovers for them to catch their breath, smoking cigarettes and drinking cocktails. There were the ones at the standing tables and closer to the bar where they waited in between dances and watched the others under the canopy and the lights that darkened the rest of the backyard, everything white where it wasn't dark. It was these parties they were all dressed up for that made someone feel like they were somewhere else, feel like they felt they were somewhere else, because the way they dressed made them look like they were and the way they danced made them look like they felt they were, the music playing through them while the black grand piano from inside sat still in its caster cups in the middle of it all.

How do you think they got the piano out here.

The one with horn-rimmed glasses shrugged and said, You

weren't at the last party were you.

I meant to, but you know. I drank some more and my hand was cold and I put the glass down. Where's Adam, I asked him while I watched most of the dancers fall off toward the patio then try to orient themselves to go back inside or look for their tables and their drinks. I told him, If there is anymore blow to go around I'll throw down for some.

Adam isn't really having any.

Okay.

What have you been up to.

I'm looking for someone who I don't know what they look like.

There were a few of them at first, buzzards circling around their table, having left their drinks there in the heat only to come back and pick through anything that still looked good, half diluted and half deluded, they were buzzing in between the standing tables and they would have to come to the bar soon enough to keep the buzz going, freshen their drinks only to leave them elsewhere.

When did you get back, he asked me.

Almost a year now.

That's alright there's been something good every weekend. The one with horn-rimmed glasses licked the length of the cigarette and stared at it then held it under his nose. It's been a while. He put a slice of lime in his drink then took another and wedged it on the rim. He started toward the standing tables and I followed him. The table was covered in empty and unempty cups, a number of beer bottles, dark stains in the white tablecloth, and everything else that was left there to come back to. I kept my drink close to the edge and away from it all. There's been something alright in between too, he finished. But I'm sure there'll be more before everyone leaves for good.

Right.

The one with horn-rimmed glasses put the rolled cigarette

in a vest pocket. Shit did you want one, he asked and reached his hand over the bulge of another pocket.

I shook my head and put my hand up no. No I need a few more drinks before I do.

He frowned while he ran his thumb and forefinger to either end of his mustache several times before bothering with his drink, only to frown again. It's the last cigarette of the year, he said. He reached into one of his pants pockets then the other but pulled out nothing.

That's good. You have to quit sometime. Why not get a head start.

I'm not quitting. He reached into one of his vest pockets and pulled out a prepackaged strip of sealed round white pills. But if I were to quit, which I wouldn't, never smoke a cigarette again for the rest of my life, but give it up altogether, that'd be so much easier. He struggled to tear two of the pills out of their plastic then looked at them in his palm before he put the rest back in one of his pants pockets. Nothing compared to smoking a few cigarettes or even just one a week, after finishing a pack or two packs in that same amount of time, now that's really something if you're not quitting altogether. He held his hand out. Do you want one.

What is it.

Nicotine lozenges.

I laughed. You're like all the stages of addiction. Beginning, end, middle.

Weren't you told to hang up your hold ups at the door.

No. I drank while he popped the lozenges into his mouth. What about my jacket.

That too, he said with his mouth full and not sounding quite like himself

I don't know. I never got addicted enough to quit, to want to quit even.

It's not hard not to get addicted to anything.

I do feel this bad comedown creeping up on me though,

cause I've been awake for so long, so do you have anything on you for that.

Hold on, he said while he had some of his drink and frowned then went through his pockets as he looked back and forth, though we were alone at our table and no one watched him. It was loud with more of them back at their tables talking and laughing again and it was hard to hear the jazz music and even the one with horn-rimmed glasses, the lozenges on his tongue or clicking against his teeth when he spoke. I leaned in closer when he held out a fist and dropped two pills into my palm and told me, Take two and see where they take you.

What is it.

For the comedown.

How much do I owe you, I asked and reached into my pants pocket.

He stopped me and waved it off then motioned for me to take the pills, so I did and we drank together and it went down well enough. Just pay me for the coke as well. I'll let you know when we do some.

Thank you doctor. I drank again and looked around but knew everyone and cleared my throat. Do those things even do anything, I asked. The lozenges.

They're a lot like cigarettes, he said and he stuck his tongue out. Much more absinthey I'd say, even help with a cough, though it's not like they coat your tongue and throat. He laughed and he coughed, but if he laughed because he coughed or coughed because he laughed I couldn't tell, but he would cough and laugh until his face turned red.

I drank and felt bad and I wanted another drink as he took another lozenge to tell me about the past month or so, all the parties that had happened and the ones that would happen, his mustache moving up and down, all of them sounding the same. Shit yeah, he would repeat whenever he remembered something good then laughed and coughed. He coughed then laughed again while we finished our drinks and he finished telling me about something. It's one of the pre-war buildings there, he said and chewed on the lime that had rested on the side of his cup.

What is.

The co-op.

Right.

You could fit a hundred people just on the balcony, and it isn't as fucking hot as it is here. He looked through some of the drinks on the table then settled on one that was mostly red with a lime in it and it didn't look too bad to drink. He seemed to like limes. Because it's so much closer to the beach. But yeah, there are more drugs there too or maybe just as much, but definitely more per capita.

Well it is a co-op after all, I said and I smiled. Whether it was because they lived in a co-op or because they lived in the city, it was the sort of interesting place where uninteresting people lived like they were interesting when they lived there, though if they didn't have the same party here in the valley every year for the past few years, they would have had it there in the co-op in the city, but traditions die hard if they're the only one. And it is Hollywood.

Westwood yeah but almost. He tasted his new drink and frowned, but not like before. It was a good frown. But yeah, you're coming to the beach tomorrow right.

The beach.

We're gonna go running on the beach tomorrow morning, and then we're going to the co-op to get ready for tomorrow night. You didn't come last year did you. We're having another party like this after this. Part two.

I think I did. Part two of the New Year's Eve party.

The after New Year's Eve party.

The New Year's after party.

Party two, part two. The New Year's party.

I hadn't heard about it this year.

Well, you're invited to both of them. I'll be the first to say it then.

The beach too, I asked and frowned. It was the only other tradition they had.

They're all trying to run to stay in shape which is funny because I'm in the best shape I've ever been in my life but they all drink and smoke more now than they ever pretended to, which I have to say is the only reason I'm going.

Yeah, I'll come and drink maybe.

Sounds good. He shook my hand and said, Maybe don't drink too much though. He found the rolled cigarette in his pocket and had some more of his red drink and left it there as he smiled his frown and said something about going to go find somewhere good for the last cigarette of the year before stopping to ask me, Did you hear Andrea died.

Yeah.

Yeah, he said and stood there for a second then turned to walk to the patio as I put my elbows down and leaned most of my weight on the table for a while to look for an unfamiliar face while trying to make sense of what some of the buzzards around me were saying.

They sounded sober and I felt the same, so I went to the bar and the bottle right where I left it and another handful of ice and poured until beige turned dark brown. The buzzards were settling in at their tables before they started heading toward me, so I left for the patio, walking along the length of the canopy, looking at the bald and round bassist and the red faced trumpeter who were both much older than the rather younger drummer everyone there knew.

All the couches and chairs that looked old enough and matched well enough, upholstered with the same cream color where they weren't wooden, had been arranged to make the patio into more of a parlor. There was a Victorian sort of sofa with some brunette already sitting there who I must have known from somewhere, but I still walked over slowly then fainted onto the end of the sofa where all the Victorian women put their feet up, spilling some of my drink between the two of us. The brunette hadn't noticed, but then again everyone was talking to someone sitting next to them. The spill sat in a small puddle on the plastic and I brushed it with my fingers until it streamed off the slipcover and slid down the end of the sofa and onto the ground as I licked my fingertips and frowned at the stained concrete.

What're you on.

They were both looking at me, the brunette smiling and the blonde who leaned over her to ask me what I was on, only to whisper something to her like I was on something, as though I couldn't tell I didn't know either of them. I straightened my tie and said, Do I like look I'm on something.

Are you on something, the brunette asked. She was beautiful with her brown eyes and her hair bent toward her neck at the ends and all her freckles, her black dress tight around her thick thighs that were crossed to hide something and show more of something else, which I could still sort of see through her black stockings, tinted but pale. There might have been some stubble there going all the way up her legs and down under her dress, which was short enough and black enough that as much as any woman would she looked just as good when she shrugged her shoulders and the straps stretched with them. Well, she asked me.

Is it any good, the blonde laughed.

I hope it's something good if it is, I said.

He's not on anything, the blonde said. The blonde was a blonde. He's just odd.

Do you not know.

Not yet, no. I smoothed my tie down my shirt and wished I wore a vest. I'm still waiting.

Maybe he is, the blonde said. It sounds like he is.

Do you think so.

What about you two.

What about us two.

Are you having a good time.

Yes.

Yeah why not.

I had some of what was left over from my fall and felt the slipcover. I asked the brunette, Did you know in France in the winter they wrap plastic around fruits on trees for them to stay good.

Who told you that, the blonde asked.

Yeah, was it a Frenchman.

No I think it was a poet.

Oh.

But it is a poetic language isn't it, French.

The blonde laughed at me. Okay.

Is it. The brunette smiled.

The music swelled behind us then there was a lull and another cadence and everyone clapped, wherever they were and whether or not they had danced, everyone clapped when they could hear the song had ended.

It is what it is, I said and my hands were too full to clap so I didn't turn to watch the same way the brunette and the blonde did before going back to themselves and talking about whatever they talked about. It had quieted down then gotten even louder with the band switching their instruments and all I could hear was the buzz of conversation and the meaninglessness of what we said so we had something to say.

I don't think so, the blonde said.

They turned back to me with smiles and I stared at where the scotch had spilled on the plastic. What are these couches made of, I asked. Stainless steel. I felt the plastic between our legs as the brunette bounced up and down. The blonde leaned farther in to feel it then sat back in her chair.

They are kind of uncomfortable.

They are, aren't they.

They finished their drinks they had kept on the ground and left me with the sofa all to myself. I watched their legs and drank and didn't feel bad that I had poured enough to stay after the spill, the length of my conversations with women I didn't know always in some proportion to the length of their legs, easier as it was to get their legs to part than to spread their lips, but then again a woman's legs are to most men what a man's face is to most women. Most of a man's life is determined by his jawline as much as most of a woman's by the seam in her stocking. I stuck my jaw out like I had nothing to say that wouldn't draw someone to hit me. I frowned then drank and moved to the other end of the sofa where they all fainted when overcome with something too much for themselves.

The band picked up where they had left off, loud and fast to keep everyone where they were. I drank slow while everyone talked or smoked, sometimes going to get something before someone else would sit where they were. I listened but still missed most of what they said and tried not to drink too much to not feel the comedown when I saw Serrano make his way to the sofa, sitting down softly to light a cigar and going through several matches until he was sure it would stay lit, the smoke billowing with several deep breaths before he spoke.

Smooth like jazz.

It started somewhere down in his throat that should have brought some smoke out with it, but he was only holding up his glass, surprised at the neatness of the dark brown drink, talking to no one but himself. His white sleeves were cufflinked passed his gray tweed, brown elbow patched jacket that his shoulders filled out, his neck thick, though he could tie a tie from memory in more ways than one and even the black bow tie he had on. He had a wide nose, short black curled hair, brown skin and thin lips and he was clean-shaven and there were several dewdrops of sweat in between the bottom of his nose and his upper lip. Everyone pronounced his name one way or another, the difference being an *an* or an *on* in Serra*n*o or Serro*n*o, but never saying which way it was himself, he would answer to either.

Let me ask you something Serrano, if a brunette asks you if you're on something, what would you, Serrono, say to her.

Yeah. He sat his drink on the ground to smoke his cigar. He closed his eyes when he smiled then he nodded at me. I'd like to be *in* something. He laughed and the smoke hiccuped loudly out of his mouth and he leaned forward to pick up his glass again and hold it up to me. He didn't say anything he didn't have to for us to drink.

Smooth like plastic, Serraño, smooth like plastique. I said it as smooth as I could, in the way some of them even added an *ñ* to his name to make him Serraño, but I was only making an ass of myself and not Serrano. If only his last name hadn't become synonymous with New Year's Eve and if only his first name wasn't harder to pronounce than his last name, though he just laughed and we both knew it sounded fake. Not the cups, I mean.

No, not the cups.

The canopy had emptied and the bar was crowded with a line to get into the crowd, two of the buzzards having gone around to tend from the back of the bar, slowing it down from self-service. I wished I hadn't spilled any of the scotch or at least that the brunette noticed I did and I wished I wouldn't have to wait for the song to slow and the crowd to clear.

It's a good thing you have these covered in plastic.

He held the cigar close to his mouth and said, Or else we'd have a casus belli.

I smiled when he shrugged.

These are out here for a reason, they would've been even if they weren't covered.

Right.

He left the cigar on his lips to flatten his nose back and forth like he was allergic to or smelled something that bothered him, the smell of the smoke or the dryness of his cologne maybe, but he stopped and looked at me. Did you know they say bulls are actually colorblind.

No.

You didn't know they say that.

No I didn't know they were colorblind.

He closed his eyes again and rested his head against the sofa back with his cigar in his mouth, holding his drink then having some before laughing again, smoky and sincere. Yeah, they are. It's not the cape being red as much as it is the cape being there and something to chase, or something to charge at rather. He drank and he forced out another laugh and held the cigar to his mouth.

I laughed too with nothing else to do, shaking the ice in my drink that was fast to water down. Serrano took the cigar from his mouth to look at the lit end, rolling it along his thumb with two fingertips from his wide hands. I had heard he had just gotten back from Spain where his family was from. I always remembered him wearing glasses, which he might have worn sometimes the same way everyone else there didn't always have to but did anyway, his eyes slits while he stared at the cigar shedding onto his clothes, his eyes red from staring hard.

Where've you been man, he asked me. When'd you get here.

Here and there, mostly here though.

Me too.

I didn't think you'd come back at all this year, Serrono.

Yeah. He had some of his drink then groaned bending over to leave it on the ground. I did get bitters. Whoever was supposed to bring them forgot to, but it was really hard to get back here. It always is with those family things, nobody there wanted me to leave. Nobody here thought I'd be back before midnight. He laughed and I looked to the bar, the line the same length as before. But I brought a bottle of something you'll like. Later though.

Yeah, the bar's crowded.

Good. He reached for his drink again. He had more in his cup than I did, but still I raised my water and waited for him to say something. To what.

To the bitter end, Serrano.

To the bitter end.

We drank and I told him, Yeah I've been drinking to excess a lot.

To excess, he repeated with his cup up again.

Yes, to excess.

Good.

We finished our drinks and he put his cup down on the concrete again. I shook the ice in mine and tilted my head back to try for something. Yeah, this summer has really turned into a yearlong summer. He sat back with his cigar and waited for me to go on, but I had nothing to drink and we listened to the buzzing for a while. But it's not like you can actually kill bulls anymore, right.

No.

Life and death.

People don't like to see the difference between life and death.

There's no use crying over spilled blood.

There isn't.

If it's covered in plastic.

He pointed at the sofa and some ash fell onto the slipcover he then brushed away. Look at this stain. We looked at whatever he was pointing at. That's been there for ten years, no one's noticed. We stared at nothing.

Right.

Serrano bent over to get his drink but stopped halfway and sat up straight. I also had nothing to drink, but it was his alcohol I wasn't drinking, not that he would keep someone from drinking, least of all if it was his alcohol, but he sort of was because he looked like he had something more to say.

Maybe I should have told him I meant I didn't think he would be back for the winter, not the other party he had gone to before midnight, but he had made it either way and he did after all have a family he was close to as much as he had friends over to his family's house even when he wasn't there. I could use another drink, I said but I didn't want to leave him behind to the mouths of the buzzards while he sat there relighting his cigar and maybe thinking he would end up dead in the pool by the end of the night. I asked him, When're you shipping off for good then.

A few months. I'm just joining the reserves though. I'm not a young man anymore.

You're too great for your own good, Serrano. Let me ask you something, what branch do you think I could get into.

The air force. He laughed. They're not as tough.

Right. I laughed.

The song ended before anyone could tell the next one by the same tempo, the drummer sitting as straight as he could be postured at the piano, the bassist down behind the drums, the trumpeter playing a saxophone in between shallower breaths, a number of dancers under the canopy but not in pairs. It was too late not to dance.

Serrano coughed and touched his nose and he coughed again and waited for the cigar to take before he turned to me and asked, You're coming to the beach tomorrow right.

I felt the slipcover while I hmmed and hummed without a trumpet at my mouth to sound good and I listened to the canopy filling to its sides again while he said something about having to take more than two cars, counting on his fingers, nine without the cigar, something about there always being someone who at the last moment would make up the difference.

I asked him, What're you on.

He could only laugh and say, Is that a yes or no then.

I shrugged and didn't have to say anything for him to think

I was a yes.

What were we talking about before, he asked.

Life and death.

We were talking about bullfighting.

What's the difference.

The ending's different now because there really isn't one. All the bulls live. It's all bullshit. It's enough to make you feel bad for them, all of them. He should have had a drink then and I should have too, the drunker one gets the more they are who they are, even when they aren't themselves. The matadors, the picadors, the banderilleros. The aficionados too, most of all though the fuckin bulls, cause they're all just fucking afraid of getting gored by a bull in front of everyone there in Pamplona. Do you know what they say that is.

I shook my head no.

Serrano laughed then stood up and raised and lowered his leg several times bending his knee like he was kicking at some dirt again and again. He touched his knee. I'm not sure what it is. My knee's been bothering me. He stood up straight. I might wrap it up for tomorrow. It'll be fine.

So what do they say it is Serraño.

Agoreaphobia.

He laughed loudly then patted me on the shoulder and left to get another drink. I stayed where we were and when I stood up again could tell how hot it still was less than an hour left before our ties would be loosened at midnight, though some of them were already jacketless with their sleeves rolled up and some of the others were back inside the house to not have to take off their jackets or have to dance. I buttoned up my jacket and walked several steps before the ground started to even out under me. My suit looked better worn altogether because the places it didn't fit right pulled at each other to make it seem like it did.

The screen door was stuck on its track and I pulled at it until a brunette was behind me, asking me how I had been and saying how good it was to see me. I got the door open and stepped to the side to let her pass through then I followed her into what looked like a model home with no furniture. Everything in the room had been moved outside, so everyone stood around and talked with drinks in their hands, some of them leaning against the counter at the end of the room and at the start of the kitchen, which had been turned into another bar, quieter there than it was outside.

I went over to the long granite countertop where there were emptied hors d'oeuvre dishes and fewer bottles than outside that would have to do to make myself a drink. The ice was colder and I had more than before, resting my elbow on the counter to listen to their buzzing as I drank. The more I listened to them the more they sounded like each other the more they talked to each other.

There were some girls across the counter from me asking how they were and saying how they looked good, though they had all started to look good by then, until one of them said she felt like dancing and they left their glasses and went and I stayed to drink. When someone would come to the counter to make a drink they would talk to me and I could tell how much more likely I was to meet some guy I sort of knew than some girl I didn't at all. I was bored with what I had to say, so I would say whatever to talk with someone when they made their drink. Drinking has brought me nothing but trouble and good times, I said to more than one. I have been alive for three days, you know. Whether it was because what I would have said was boring or because I had said it enough times to make it sound boring, if they were to put everything back together I said to each of them that night about what I did or was doing or going to do, it would be nonsense, but nonsense made sense one at a time.

Adam came into the room from the hallway that ran toward the front of the house, smiled and came over to me, looked at my drink, smiled again and squeezed my shoulder.

What're we drinking for auld lang syne, something simple.

Something brown.

Something big and brown and beautiful.

I do love a brunette with a body.

Easy on the eyes, hard on the cock.

I laughed and I said, It's hard sometimes to tell the difference between brunettes and redheads.

Adam went around the counter and I followed him into the kitchen where he grabbed a glass, rinsed it in the sink, filled it with as much ice as he had before then feeling the bottles to maybe see their vintages through their shapeliness took his time turning the bottles this way and that. It wasn't that crowded the way everyone was coming in and out and looking for somewhere else to go, so I didn't mind staying there as I filled my glass with ice. He went through the bottles again then asked me what I was drinking.

Something scotch.

Yeah, alright. He found the brown bottle where I had left it and poured for both of us, holding his glass up in one motion to drink then hold it against his cheek. So do you think you're going to the beach tomorrow.

Serrano already got to you too then.

Serrono did.

I think I am. I had some of my drink and he nodded and looked at some girls that had come in then he switched to the other cheek to stare and he grabbed an empty beer bottle from the counter as he stared through it like a scope to say some brunette looked good. His face was red and round and I asked him, Are you going.

Yeah me too. He put the bottle down to run his sleeve over his forehead then examine it. I'm gonna end up staying here tonight cause I don't have a ride until tomorrow morning, but why not though. We have to live a little more. He grabbed my shoulder and asked me, Why are you here.

I don't know. I drank. Why are you here.

No, why are you here.

Why am I not.

We moved to the end of the room to look outside. Adam handed me his drink and pulled at the screen door until it closed, took his cup and switched it back and forth from time to time, looking at the girls outside like they couldn't see him and the girls inside since he could see them better.

They all look good to me, I said. The way they look good when you kinda know you wouldn't want to know how they look if you could tell the difference between them at midnight, you drink and you're okay knowing that the way they look right now, that they do and they don't really look like that at all.

None of us look the way we do right now. He looked back and forth and I saw how there was a wrinkle to my jacket that had the left shoulder looking shorter than the right one, but then again Adam didn't look too good in his suit either. Man.

We drank and looked at the girls outside.

How do you think they got the piano outside.

Adam felt his cheeks. When I was working for these movers in New York, my friend who got me the job told me about a piano that was inside this apartment in the Village for several decades. They'd done all this construction around it, but the people moving in wanted it out, and when my friend was there he said they couldn't. It had to have been brought in on a crane. They couldn't get it out without having to take down at least four walls, so what they ended up doing is just sawing it in half to get rid of it.

That's wild. I laughed. Was it a grand piano or, I guess it doesn't make much of a difference. I couldn't see the piano behind the buzzards circling in pairs under the canopy. There is something about jazz music that really makes people think like they're in the jazz age, not the golden age of jazz, but the jazz age.

We drank and looked at the girls inside.

Everybody is fucking everybody, I said after a while.

Who's everybody.

Everybody here.

Well, they're all dressed up and their hair's done up, it's the hair that does it, the first thing you see about them, fuckin hair, the way it looks if it looks good, if it doesn't. Of course, it's the other things too, their tits and their asses, which is really just determined by whether your mother held you more or you had to pull on her skirt for her to hold you, tits or ass. And their legs, well, legs are really only legs because of where they end, the better the longer it takes them to get there.

The better to see them.

Like everything else, but it's their long hair, because you think of them as being brunettes and blondes and redheads. It's not so much the one with the nice ass as it is the brunette with the nice ass, right.

Secondary sex characteristics are everything.

That's it.

Sounds too true to be true, I said but laughed when I saw the brunette with the nice ass he was talking about. But it sounds good.

Adam shrugged and held his cup up to his cheek and said nothing.

I don't think I really know anyone here. You know what you were saying, we might as well be dead, if we were in some war, so many of us wouldn't have come back, we'd be better off, it'd be better off for everyone and everyone else. It's neither here nor there now, but it's like, who in the fuck are all these motherfucks.

I had had a few more drinks in the half hour and I felt good. There was nothing but what was red, my eyes closed but the light staining them, nothing else to do but step step side-step and step step side-step until I saw them all at once when I blinked my eyes open again, her even more than the rest of them, the song not too sudden that we weren't spinning closer together and back and forth that I might have fallen over if we weren't. We were close enough for me to speak into her mouth and for her to smile and mouth that she couldn't hear me.

Audra came in closer as I went to her ear to tell her something, combing her hair to curl back behind her ear for her to hear me better, only to bite her earlobe. She pulled away and squinted at me then tightening her lips together and pulling them to the side showed off her one dimple. Her hair was short around her ears but grown out from when it was shaved on the side, brushed to the left on top, reddish brown still from when it used to be brownish red, her face rounded with high enough cheekbones blushed several times lighter than her lips were red. She was wearing a white dress and she pushed her thigh up between my legs and I could kiss her right then.

The song ended with some applause and she stuck her hand between my clapping and stopped me from starting again, holding my hand to lead me from under the canopy and out to the bar before anyone else got there. She always led me somewhere good when she held my hand.

What'll it be, she asked.

No, I said because I wouldn't have as much to drink as I did the last time with her. You.

Huh.

Pick your poison, I'll have the same.

How romantic.

She was the sort of person that alcohol brought the best out of but never did often enough. We drank well together if not too much. She picked up and put down the menu but didn't know what she wanted then went through the bottles like she wanted all of them. Alcohol made us the same. I ran two scissor fingers through her hair to see how much longer it was around her ears since the last time I breathed into them and bit her earlobe while she held my hand up the stairs and down the hall, passing the drunks I didn't know then, the doors painted into an eastern sort of pantheon, lifting her onto her loft bed as she leaned back for me to pull off her pants then she put her thighs on my shoulders and crossed her legs around my neck to press my tongue to her pussy.

A gin and tonic sounds good.

Sure, I said and picked up the menu. Let me just see what goes into it.

Shut up. She wrestled the menu away from me and I took a new cup for her and the gin bottle and she handed me another cup. Two gin and tonics.

What, two for me and two for you. I grabbed two more. I think you've had enough, but okay.

She took them from me, One for you and me.

Just the one, I asked. You're right, you've had enough. This is your last one before I cut you off for good. I smiled and poured the gin evenly into the cups and I cut a lime into wedges while she emptied some from hers into mine. It didn't matter which one of us drank more as long as both of us drank.

She filled the cups with ice and I saw how small her hands were and I saw how short and how small she was too. I dropped the limes in as she poured the tonic water and poured it to the top of her cup and I held our drinks then handed hers to her when we reached the end of the backyard.

The jazz band was playing a song that sounded too orchestral for the three of them. She stood close enough to me that when I watched them play I could still see when she drank.

I think I'm in the middle of this sort of midlife crisis, I said.

You're not even twenty-three years old though, aren't you.

Yeah, no. But how do you think I feel, along with the whole midlife crisis, knowing I'm going to die when I'm not even forty-six years old.

She looked away to smile like she did when I hadn't tried too hard for her to smile. She didn't seem drunk and she didn't talk like we were in bed but like we never were.

I like your hair brushed to the left, I said.

My right.

Your right, my wrong.

She stared at me.

Is your hair red.

No.

It looks red.

Maybe it's the light.

Right.

Her bed smelled good like her and the sheets were warm too. She had said she always slept on the side closer to the edge but I was scared she might fall off. She was quicker to have something to say when she wasn't sober and she couldn't lie still either, turning around to face me from time to time, breathing into my mouth, always looking away when she smiled. There was nothing left to do but lie in bed and tell each other some truth.

Do you ever think about all the things you could say in a moment like this, from whenever the moment is, from several years ago, even if it hasn't happened yet, whenever it might be from. I'm always thinking about that, speaking for both parts in my head again and again, thinking of what I might say or might have said. She turned onto her side and pressed up against me. I don't know if that sounds dumb now that I think about it. She was softer and I felt the thin, almost blonde hairs nearly shaved on the back of her head before she turned the light off and I couldn't see if she had pulled her lips to the side to show her one dimple anymore. I always sound more eloquent in the fake conversations I make up in my head.

It doesn't sound dumb at all. I told her I knew what she meant. God writes such bad dialogue.

She fell asleep before I did and I felt the bones in her back but woke up before she did and got out of bed and dressed while she was still naked and I felt bad for not fucking her after how hard we tried with our hands and mouths before her nose started to bleed, which she said was normal, not normal, but normal for her, nothing to do with the half hard dick down her throat, but not far down enough. She left to clean herself and I went after her to clean what must have been the only bit of blood that had flown from my head down, walking into several other rooms before I found hers again and got into bed and we got over feeling embarrassed together.

The jazz band came to a decrescendo and she asked me, What're you gonna do then.

I don't know.

About your midlife crisis.

I'm not sure if it's a midlife crisis really. I think I might be suffering from one of those psychosomatic sorts of things.

I don't think there's anything somatic about what you're suffering from.

I laughed then I told her, I'm thinking I might run away from home.

I don't think men in their early twenties can actually run away from home.

Because they're all afraid to, this generation of manchilds. Manchildren. Menchildren. I'm not sure which one. The buzzards were where we left them under the canopy and I watched her drink and I knew why they danced. The waiting was getting good. I should have fucked her when I had the chance. How nice she looked in her dress. I had waited much too much. The closer one gets, I said. The better the waiting gets too. I don't know what I'm saying.

Do you ever.

I think I'm suffering from psychosis of the liver.

Oh really.

But I don't know how you could be self-aware and not need a drink. There were pauses when we spoke, not to think about what someone said, to think of something to say. I might be crazy, I don't know. I think I've been awake for three days.

Why.

I can't remember.

Are you trying to remember.

Not really, no.

Did you know they say the two most common cases for people checking into mental asylums think they're either the Devil or Jesus Christ. Like, they believe they're either one or the other.

I don't think I'm either.

That's good.

Let me ask you something. If you didn't have such a difficult time remembering your dreams, don't you think it wouldn't be that hard to dismiss your waking life.

She didn't say anything and had some of her gin.

What is that, a white dress.

It is.

It isn't the light making it look white.

What are you talking about.

I don't know. How's life, how's love, how's your love life.

I'm sort of seeing someone.

That's never stopped me.

You're gonna end up all alone.

Maybe, but I don't think I could be with anyone that puts their needs ahead of mine.

Of course not, that's because you're you. You know

women release this chemical oxytocin when they're with someone. It's what makes them sink their claws and teeth into someone and not want to let go.

I could go for some OxyContin.

Do you have some on you, she asked and she bit her lip then showed her one dimple again.

She always bit her lip when she wanted something she didn't want. When I bit her small nipples they reddened and she said to stop, so I breathed onto them like I might bite them again. I laughed and I kissed them and kissed her and I covered her breasts with my hands.

You don't think they're small do you.

No, I like them. They're the great plains.

Shut up.

They're great and there's nothing plain about them.

In the morning I looked at the slab of mirror on the ground that had been stood up against her armoire and one of the corners was broken into several shards. I leaned it up again and threw the handful of glass away. Her nipples had purpled and I was harder from waking up than at anytime the night before when she had her hands on my stomach and her mouth on me. She asked me if I was Jewish and I said I was a Zionist. In the morning I covered her in her blanket and left.

Well, do you have some.

What.

OxyContin.

Not on me, no.

In you.

Yeah.

Okay.

What are those, blue eyes.

What. Why do you keep asking me things like that.

I don't know. Sometimes I'm not so sure I see everything the same as everyone else, so I try to make sure I do. Do you know what I mean, see there's this reality, right, and I have to be sure I'm seeing the same one as you. Like, what is that, a gin and tonic.

God.

Yeah.

Where are you gonna go when you go.

I don't know.

Who are you going with.

Adam.

I don't think I know Adam.

You'd like him. He's one of the good ones.

I feel the worst. She rubbed the side of her head. Do you have a cigarette.

I don't think so. I patted down my pockets. No.

Well then, you know what, we're through.

We never started.

This is over.

We were never under.

Whatever. She looked away then back to me. I'll be right back.

Audra turned to go and her white dress looked thin on her body in the light from the canopy, her hair longer than it used to be, not looking as good as I remembered. Most of life was looking for something to say or something to put in one's mouth. How many of them she had fucked had to have been any number of them in the co-op who had horn-rimmed glasses and thin mustaches and were her type. I waited for her to go inside before I left the end of the backyard and felt bad for not fucking her before all of them who had had.

Come on fucker we're gonna do another line, the one with horn-rimmed glasses said with a hand on my back until we reached the hallway and I followed him and turned the corner at the end not to the left and outside to the front yard but to the right to go upstairs again. We passed a couple and I tried not to stare at the strapless blonde in between floors and on top of some jacketless no one I knew, but when we went into the room at the end I could still see her tongue in his mouth with the door open, so I locked it behind me but could still hear the party buzzing outside.

Everyone was there again. Serrano in white briefs with his thumb on his lips looking over all the changes of clothes he had laid on one side of his bed, he couldn't convince himself on what to choose after already wearing two of his better outfits, the rest of them a mess after Adam pushed them aside to lie down on the other side of the bed. Adam held his hands to his cheeks then in his mouth, staring at the ceiling fan, feeling his teeth and mouthing some words. The one with horn-rimmed glasses stood over an open drawered dresser and cut the lines while the other two stared over his shoulder, nothing to say to either of them, with every line someone else being told about the cocaine. There was the one with the shaved head who looked like one of those phrenological figureheads and he talked in long circles and had as much to say as last time all over again to another listener, this time the one with his life determined by his jawline. His smiles were wide and his teeth stretched to fill them and he was the opposite of the one with the shaved head, the phrenological figurehead in brown and white, the listener in black on black, the one with a round skull in which I could see the worst parts of myself, the other with a square jawline. They talked over the party.

You smell the drug and it takes you somewhere right away, while that feeling takes you somewhere else, it's all in a kind of feeling, the touching feeling and the smelling, the smelling and the touching feeling. The figurehead rubbed his thumb against the rest of his fingers then pressed it to his middle finger in front of their faces and snapped several times and the two of them laughed. That feeling is the feeling you're feeling.

My heef feel humb. Adam sat up in the bed with a few fingers still in his mouth. Hoo hor heef heel hat hall hum right now. He wiped his hand on his pants and said, I don't need any painkillers with this. I can't feel anything.

The figurehead and the other one shrugged, looking over the shoulders of the one with horn-rimmed glasses then back and forth to each other and Adam again.

Hi hunno hoh they hay hohaine. Don't they say it's cut with something by the time it gets here.

They say lots of things though don't they.

They have to say something, I said.

They say they say when they have to say something to keep the mouth moving. So they don't feel dumb and so they don't feel numb.

Novocaine, Serrano said and pointed at Adam. Is the new cocaine.

Hohaine heh heh hoo hohaine, naga.

Naga.

Yeah, naga.

Naga y pues nada.

They laughed and the one with horn-rimmed glasses put the small white bag back into another vest pocket and asked if anyone had a cigarette. He looked at me and I went through my pockets then at Serrano who went through the pairs of pants he had on the bed until he found a pack to toss to him. The one with horn-rimmed glasses took one of the cigarettes and tapped the end of it into the start of one of the lines, rolling up the twenty I had given him, had his line then looked to the figurehead to take the bill and tighten it again before he bent over the dresser to have his and hand it to the other one to do the same.

They thay hickory reheats his self. Adam wiped his mouth with the back of his hand and again ran both of them down to his knees and stood up and took the bill to have his line before handing it to me tightly rolled but too thin. They say history repeats itself.

History repeats itself as long as historians repeat themselves that history repeats itself.

They say the past is the past too.

So they don't feel dumb and so they don't feel numb.

Being dumb is more than having nothing to say, nada.

More or less.

The lines looked long and good on the short brown dresser and it wasn't too hard to tell what was dust and what was worth snorting since their handprints to wipe the dresser were still there at the end where they snorted. I could taste the drip from last time and I ran my tongue over the roof of my mouth. I rerolled and tightened the twenty the way I had been shown the first time I covered my left nostril and breathed through the right, going down to the end of the line then up to close my eyes and cover my nose and breathe nothing. It smelled the way it always smelled.

The hole has to be large enough for it to get through, Angel had told me.

Angel was in his early thirties and looked much older than he was, the cocaine having thinned him out enough through the years to look like he took good care of himself for his age. He had a drugged up smile but other than that it was hard to tell him apart from everyone he sold to. Angel had sold me on the time it took.

It'll leave your system in three days, he said with nostrils flared to snort a thin line. I'm always selling to the military here for the weekend.

Something not being there in three days was enough reason to do anything.

What do you think.

Serrano held up two white shirts, his stomach standing out almost as much as the muscles in his arms, looking unlike himself outside of a suit he always looked like he was born wearing. He must have been asking me, but I couldn't tell the difference. They were both white.

The three days was how I sold Serrano on it the first time. He had rolled his pant legs up and slipped his feet into the pool at the end of the night. He told me, I only ever write when I write to women I'm into. Poetry.

I was the opposite in the only suit I owned, my legs folded under me. I told him, I don't know what to say unless I'm on something.

I didn't say that doesn't help.

I find it easier to talk to women when I'm not entirely sure they exist.

He laughed hard.

I'm okay. He saw the rolled up twenty but just waved me off. He stared at the shirts and he mumbled to himself, no one else making a move for the line. Too much on my mind, he said.

They say the past is the past, but the past is the past they say.

That's the line of the night, nada.

No, that is.

You're going into the future so the past is farther and farther away, but at the same time you're also going into the past and then going even farther to reach the past, so it takes longer to get to it and faster because you're bouncing back and forth both ways.

The last line on the dresser and all the dust around it looked good. Everything was cut smaller and smaller until there was nothing to snort. I tightened the twenty with my forefinger and thumb covering either end.

Diminishing returns, Angel always said.

Angel was born somewhere in Spain but said he didn't have an accent like his father did. His father held several patents for his work in the hills overlooking Berkeley in the material sciences and other sorts of matters unknown to most men.

It's going to be in the smallness of things that everything's going to end, Angel said.

I didn't know what to say, so I said nothing.

Everything is going to fold in on itself, he said while he folded his hands together with fingers interlocked but didn't say whether it was his father that told him that or not. All he had ever done in his life was be born to his father.

I snorted another line and listened to him go on.

You don't see these things, you know. You know they say the Indians couldn't see the Spaniard ships off the coast cause they hadn't seen anything like them before. They couldn't make sense of them, so they couldn't see them.

That's fucking wild, I said. But you know it's the same with the horses. They hadn't seen men like Cortés riding horses, so they thought they were horsemen. They thought they were gods.

It was a long thin line that took some time to get to the end, but when I got there it was good. I licked my fingertips to run them over the dresser and all the leftovers from the lines and licked them again. I couldn't feel my teeth.

Did you hear Andrea died, the figurehead asked me.

No.

Yeah, nada. She died like three days ago in a fucking car crash.

Jesus fuck.

Didn't you fuck her, the one with horn-rimmed glasses asked me.

Yeah, well sort of, no. She just gave me head, but I fingered her too. But that was like six or seven years ago.

I heard she was a lesbian, the other one said.

I didn't know that.

Aren't all women.

Men too.

Everyone's gay.

You're gay.

Fuck you, nada.

What do you think, Serrano asked. He was smiling, having settled on one of the white shirts he half buttoned down from the collar to his stomach, holding up two ties to the figurehead and the other one, both black but different patterns. It was the first thing they didn't agree on, so Serrano held them up to me and I shrugged.

I don't know, nada.

Serrano held his thumb to his chin and his fingers to his lips, the tie still in his hand, then the same with the other, maybe smelling them. I could taste the drip as he continued to dress himself while the one with horn-rimmed glasses and the figurehead and the other one drank. Adam sat down at the edge of the bed and wiped the saliva off his fingers then rubbed his cheeks and stood up.

I'm gonna go outside, he said.

How much longer til midnight.

Less than an hour.

A little less than half an hour.

Less than an hour then, yeah.

I think I'll go with you, I said. I'm gonna go drink until I'm drunker than I am.

Adam had some trouble with the door and I handed the bill back to the one with horn-rimmed glasses and we were out soon enough, closing the door behind us and going downstairs again, the couple having moved up a few steps from before. There were more of them inside and I followed Adam to the counter in the kitchen, loud as it was inside without the jazz music as it was outside, looking for something to drink, some of the buzzards mistook us for bartenders, so we poured the same scotch we drank in dirty glasses without ice for them until there was a lull and we left to go down the hallway again and outside to the front yard. The door had been left open and there were some of them already there sitting crosslegged in a circle in the driveway and passing something around without hearing how loud they were. The grass was dry in the front yard and we walked to the street where it wasn't as dark, the light from the streetlamps making shadows around our feet. Adam had a pack of cigarettes and separated a few of them out with his thumb and I took one.

When'd you get these.

When we got here, I don't know. He took one as well. That nada said he was quitting tonight.

Right. I laughed.

Do you have a lighter.

No.

Adam went over to the ones sitting in the circle. There were two short palm trees at the end of the driveway that seemed to come out of the same thick trunk. I sat down on the curb and put my cup just off the driveway and where the gutter started. Adam came back and lit our cigarettes and went to the others again who asked him for cigarettes, so he left the pack with one of them, walking down the driveway and past me to leave his drink on the trunk of a beige sedan. He walked a few feet into the street and his shadow went back and forth with him, ahead of him when he went the one way then falling behind him when the lamplight from across the street turned the shadow the other direction as he went back to his drink.

I had a good long drag and drank before I let go of the smoke through my nose with a shorter drag and out through my mouth. It was thick and went to my head but went well with the scotch. I like these, I think they're mostly tobacco. I held the cigarette up to the light. I'm not sure if they really are, but I've heard them say they are. Full-bodied. I love a brunette with a body.

Adam stopped a few feet away from me and stared at the ground in front of him. I don't know what I'm doing, I don't even fuckin smoke. He threw the cigarette down and went to the trunk to finish his drink. Fuck, nada.

What about the Indians. I held the cigarette to my mouth. You can't just leave that there.

Oh my bad, Sitting Bull. He held his hands up and backed away from me and went over to the cigarette, stepping on then twisting the butt into the ground before he dropped one of his hands to his side. How. He put his hand on his heart. I pledge allegiance to the pack of the Natural Spirits of America.

I did the same holding my cigarette between my middle and forefinger. I watched Adam walk back and forth again. It always looked the same in the valley with the usual two columns of cars parked along the sides of the street.

I don't think I'll go to the beach tomorrow, I said.

I feel like I'm a few years late to all of this. I've just caught up to everyone else how they were a few years ago. Now all I wanna do is drink and smoke, the way they all were back then. I don't want to be anything more than how they were.

It's never too late to recapture their youth. This is the time and place for that. I didn't know if I was or wasn't or wished I were or weren't like them, but Adam never felt one way or another for too long, so I encouraged him. You should do whatever you wanna do. Live your life a little.

Adam pulled at the thin hairs of his neckbeard. That's all there is though, you see, nothing else but the drinking or the smoking or the drugs and the girls, that's all you can be sure about. It's not so much a pleasure in those things, but the sensation you get from them, when there's nothing but your senses, but if you can't even be sure about those, when you've gone too far into the deep end and all you can be sure of is who the fuck you are, who the fuck am I, you see what I'm saying, it isn't anything else that it's all about, man.

He was drunk, but it wasn't the drinking that made him drunk, no, drinking only ever sobered him up from his natural state.

Let me have a bit of that cigarette, he said.

I handed it to him and said, Fuck or get fucked up or whatever.

Prepackaged feel good feel bad fuckeduppedness, he said as he took a drag and exhaled. Pass me some of that laudanum, nada.

Fuck some shit up, I said and took a drink then gave him the rest to finish.

This is why it all makes sense to me now. I didn't get it until a few years later, how you could feel everything you needed to feel from this, but now, fuck, of course I wouldn't wanna be much more than my extremities.

Adam stared down the street a while then looked at me, so I stood up and spat in the street and stared at my feet in the lamplight and I saw crickets there like I had in the middle of the night once around a tree trunk, but I couldn't remember when I had seen them and how old I was. I might have been three when I was chasing the crickets around the tree.

There was that and there was a year and not too long ago in the middle of the night in October when the Orionids were supposed to shower Orion that Eve and I spent the night in the grass and waited for them. Even if three days felt to me like a lifetime there were only a few days that were ever good enough to remember from time to time because most of the time one only ever thought about one or two days for most of their life. Lying there with Eve in the grass in the middle of the night had to be one of them. Eve.

Adam started to walk inside but then stopped and waited for me. There was always something we were supposed to be doing, but then again there was something to not knowing what it might be before we went about doing what we were supposed to do and we became what we were supposed to be. Adam said to me, I'm gonna go smoke whatever they're smoking.

Okay.

See you tomorrow then, nada.

I laughed and I said, I think I will go to the beach tomorrow.

Yeah. So the Chateau Marmont next week, or even the week after, but sometime before everyone is gone for good.

The handful of us at the end of the backyard with Serrano were everyone.

We have to get one of their suites for the night, which'll run us each a hundred or so or maybe less, if there are more of us, but I'm not sure about that right now.

Everyone wasn't everyone.

Let's say a hundred each with some more on the side to have enough for everyone to drink.

Someone might have said something if Serrano didn't hold up his drink and we all drank. He took his time with the little left of his cigar, having settled on a tuxedo that had him look the part for the time of night. He let go of as thick of a mouthful of smoke as his lungs could. We were all in the waiting room with him.

There has to be something to this, having what's essentially a cock in your mouth as a man.

There's nothing gayer than male heterosexuality.

It's castrating though, slowly shriveling up in your mouth as you smoke. He stared at the cigar then started up again. Come on, for something like this you all have that kind of money, it's what you think of when you think of Los Angeles, everything. Everything that's happened there, think about it, we would have been there too and we'll be talked about the same, that one night we had at the Chateau Marmont.

We have to go there to be there, the figurehead agreed.

I don't know how we haven't all stayed there already.

Me neither, one of them said.

This is the last chance though. I know I'm not coming back in the summer.

I drank to look up at the palm trees and the night, the jazz music quieting down with my back to the canopy, but less buzz than before. There was a hand on my back and I turned my head one way and the other and there was the one with horn-rimmed glasses, a cigarette on his mouth and another lit in his hand, which he traded to me for my drink as I made room for him in the circle.

And this fuck is fleeing the country to go to France.

The one with horn-rimmed glasses laughed then asked me, Are we talking about the Chateau Marmont again.

Yeah. I breathed in the short cigarette and the one with horn-rimmed glasses gave me back my drink and I patted him on the shoulder when he frowned. You're gonna live in France, I asked.

Yeah.

Do you speak French.

As long as I'm in debt.

Nothing but debt and taxes.

Not if I die.

I'm also living on borrowed time, in that I only have so much time before I have to pay back what I borrowed.

Take the money and run to France. You couldn't ever come back, but still.

There was the muted horn drawl like a capped bullhorn as the jazz band crescendoed closer to being done for the night. Most of my drink was still there, so I drank.

And Adam, is Adam even here, who knows when or if we'll ever see him again.

I thought he was expatriating like me.

I'm gonna end up on the other side of the country too, one of them said.

I think he said he's going to South America.

Yeah, Florida.

Well either way it's the last we'll see of him.

Aaron'll be here, another one said.

Maybe.

Who, Adam.

Yeah you will.

He's a good guy.

He told me he's looking for some gold or something.

If we ever knew someone who somehow disappeared in the jungle in the middle of the night.

The Everglades.

Yeah that would be Adam.

He was lost looking for the tree of life.

Why's that.

If you're ever feeling down, need to have a drink, even if he's hungover or half dead, Aaron'll finish the bottle before you.

Wait, what does that leave you to drink.

The fountain of youth I think he said.

Who's to say it isn't there, all we've ever known is there's nothing here.

You're right, Serrano laughed. Maybe he's not that good a guy.

There were two Aarons and one of them wasn't there. I didn't know which one they were talking about, so I drank and agreed with them.

I'm not too sure it isn't here, the one with horn-rimmed glasses said. I'd stay if I could.

It's gotta be somewhere, but maybe he'll find some lost gold.

I don't think Adam could pay off how much he owes me.

Me neither.

I don't think he owes you as much as he owes me.

Aaron'll sell a painting or two within the year, then die from some overdose and sell his other four hundred paintings for much more than the first two were worth. Serrano held his cigar and drink together to pull at his collar while we laughed.

Fuck, the best I could do is die, and it's already taken.

The one with horn-rimmed glasses frowned then told me, Maybe next year.

Maybe.

We should go snort something.

Or something.

Sure.

Do you have anymore of anything.

Yeah in a bit.

Think about it though, you wake up in the morning, go out onto the balcony and see someone already starting up a cigarette, maybe have a little hair of the dog, then you see the entire city the way it's meant to be seen, the last time. We'll go out and have something to eat, maybe even have another drink before we do.

It's good to always be somewhere between aperitif and digestif.

Some of them laughed while some of them drank.

We'll have a nice steak then and nothing else.

More of them laughed.

There is nothing quite like a good cut of meat, as hungover as I know we'll be in the morning, it's all we need as men, not just as men, but animals. It's what we're meant to have because we're meant as animals to go after other animals. So we'll have a good cut of animal.

They didn't have to use their words.

And that'll be the end of it. Nothing else to say, stomachs full, mouths shut.

Being a man is being an animal.

A man is nothing more than what he needs.

Which is to eat.

And to fuck.

This fucker.

Which is what we're supposed to do.

He used to have to kill to do either of those.

We're all just these sort of fucking fucks now.

Something's missing yeah.

Which is why we go to the Chateau Marmont next week.

You know what we should really do, I asked and finished

my drink. What we should really do is go fishing. I've been thinking about trying to get something good like that together for a while. I wished I still had something to drink to think of what it was that was good, but I couldn't think of it over the buzzing in the backyard. You know what I mean. I looked back at the canopy and I saw there was no one dancing, but the jazz band still played, looking like it didn't matter that all they were doing was playing for no one. I couldn't say what it was, how something like a trumpet and bass and drums could all come together to make something like jazz, but there it was. Something where you'd stand back and look at what you've done and all you know is that you've done something good.

They all agreed because we were talking the way we always were then they quieted down and that was all there was to it. I had said what there was to say and I didn't want to undo it by saying something else. They drank and I would step back to go to the bar, but I didn't, looking at all they had done in the time we were there, the others too, some of them having undone and redone their ties, their ties down to their pants and their pants pulled up to their waists, that much closer to the time they could undo them all again.

It isn't about doing something anymore, it's about doing anything now, even if there isn't a real reason to ever go to South America or somewhere else, other than everyone saying there are a lot of things to do there and lots of things to eat or to fuck, there's going down the Amazon or the Seine to the rainforest or whatever, looking for lost gold the conquistadors left, maybe it isn't there, no, it isn't there for sure, it's not about doing any one of those things, it's about doing anything.

So you'll be dead in a year after all, one of them said.

They laughed and I did too.

We're already going to the beach anyways.

That's true.

What we should do is get an amphora to drink from, drinking wine like fucking madness, it'll be all these women and wine everywhere, bacchanalia man.

Bacchanal.

You do know they say that the alcohol content was so much lower then that they had to drink more, so it's not the same as how much we drink. We could drink Dionysus under the table.

Thank the lord god Dionysus, Serrano said and they drank with their heads tilted back.

Thank Bacchus. Some of them drank again.

Thank God for the lord. No, thank the gourd.

The buzzards came out from the house into the backyard again and circled around the drunks, but it was about time, though I still didn't know if we would go next week or the week after or at all to the Chateau Marmont.

I think I'm gonna go get something to drink or something.

The one with horn-rimmed glasses shook my hand to give me three pills that looked different from before and he smiled.

My comeuppance, I asked him.

Yeah.

Take three and see where they take me, right.

Right on.

I went to the bar and put the short stub of a cigarette out in a leftover drink, not bothering with the ice water in the buckets, most of the brown bottles still good, the time of night for drinks to be straight. I had the pills with the same scotch I had all night. It must have been about midnight because the canopy had been emptied out and most of them had moved to the front of the backyard and applauded the jazz band once more, talking and laughing louder than before, then the canopy lights were turned off and the backyard went dark. Some of them screamed and others laughed at them until there was nothing but their buzzing as they walked to the end of the backyard, more of them coming from inside the house as they all moved to where it was darkest. I couldn't see what it was but started over to where the others were and could tell I was walking sort of sideways, but everyone was leaning into each other, so I didn't stand up straight but instead drank enough to be sure I wouldn't spill.

Someone said something then there was a warm body against me that was tall and thin and in the dark looked spotted like a leopard. I couldn't see her then her voice whined out of thin purple lips that were wide as I got used to the dark and saw she still didn't look the way she was.

Who are you, I asked and felt out for her.

Amanda, duh.

Amandada, I asked.

Amanda.

Amandada.

She put her body against mine and asked me, Remember when you called me a bitch.

What, when.

Last year.

I don't remember last year. I don't remember this year. I've been alive for all of three days.

Do they say that about me.

I don't think anybody says anything about you.

You're such a dick.

Anything bad I mean.

You're still a dick. She laughed and I did too.

You're such a bitch. I laughed and she left her mouth open. I didn't mean that.

I hate it when you call me that.

Oh come on I didn't mean it last year either.

You did.

I don't even think I was here last year.

You don't seem to be here this year.

No I'm not. Amandada is such a nice name anyways. Does

anyone call you Amy for short.

No.

Is it because you're so tall.

Thank you.

She must have been the same height as me if her heels didn't sink her into the grass some.

You know, it's weird, you. Most women wish they were taller, so they all wear high heels, but most tall women wish they were shorter so they could wear higher heels. You're something else.

I'm not like most women.

No you are not.

I like to be tall.

You're already so tall.

I like towering over men.

You're the tops, you're the Tower of Babel.

She leaned her head on my shoulder and I brushed her short brown hair back behind her ear.

I like that about you.

She was thin and her leopard skin dress was tight on her body.

You're an animal.

She leaned into me.

Don't fall. It'll be a long one.

That gives you more time to catch me.

We were all crowded around and they said to move farther to the end and started pushing until we all started saying to move and pushed until we moved together, waiting for whatever that was going to happen to happen before midnight. I held onto Amanda with my drink, shuffling around until she stood in front of me. I reached around to her stomach and pulled her back to me and she moved her ass back and forth and I handed her my cup and she had some, laughing when I rested my chin on her shoulder and kissed her neck up to her ear.

There was one at first that lit up with a bang, everything else quieting down while it moved by itself in the dark, back and forth where there was nothing else, red and leaving red trails from the light that came off it, nothing but its redness. Another one lit up close to it with the same bang as it began to move the same way as the first one moved back and forth and red, brighter in the light coming off both of them, the second one then moving in circles, but as soon as one did, the other did the same, spinning toward each other until the sound they made started to burn softer and the buzzing started up and the laughter again. It was black and red flickering white and blue. Another one lit up and another one after it, back and forth and up and down, circling one by one, the tops of the flames crackling as more of them banged then turned into drifting fireflies buzzing like cicadas in the middle of the night. They burned brighter as I drank and got used to the dark and I saw the ends they were on and the hands that held them, the faces in the light, the shadows in the dark to make their faces turn yellow and red, unlike themselves. I couldn't tell who they were in the light with their faces and their bodies and what they wore. I could see all of them, no one I knew, until all the fires went out without a sound and I couldn't see how dark it was because it was too bright when they were there.

She said something, but I was already headed back inside. It had gotten to my stomach sooner than I had known and I tried not to think about it, trying to drink it down, but the vomit was there the entire time. I was out of the crowd and through the bit of grass and the canopy and patio, how small it all was, walking as straight as I ever had through the open screen door, the emptied room to the long hallway and the front of the house. I tried the bathroom at the front but there was light coming out from under the door and there was no time, vomiting into my mouth and swallowing it down again, good until it came up again worse and more than before. I ran upstairs and turned the corner of the stairhead and into the room at the end and passed the dresser into the bathroom. I felt for the light switch and there it was. I vomited once into the sink then I made it to the toilet and lifted the cover, bent over for the longest time, the water sitting still with nothing in it. There were roses growing out of the off-white molding and painted on the brownish wall, pink and red and white with green stems, growing out of each other, painted in impasto brushstrokes, but then I saw there were lines where the wallpaper didn't really fit together and I vomited again. It made a sound against the water unlike piss or shit, the sound of the toilet being used for the wrong end, the white rim around the red. I sat down next to the toilet and felt good enough to try a few more times, but there was nothing left.

Maybe if there were some great end to everything we were right then and maybe if there were some casus belli to begin it, some great war we could have been drafted into, if we died or didn't, we would have come back from it knowing what we were supposed to do. I could hear them outside and they were loud, a lost generation, a whole generation wishing they were somewhere else but not where they were supposed to be. I could hear the sound of gunfire from somewhere, so it must have been midnight, but I didn't stand up and run toward it and I didn't hide from it either, but I did nothing, not knowing what I was supposed to do.

Our casus belli was there wasn't one.

I came downstairs again feeling better than before, though my mouth was dry, so I started toward the kitchen to get water or something to drink, keeping my head down to make sure my feet went one in front of the other then the other in front of the one until I reached the sink and I turned the faucet on to drink several handfuls then wash my face as the water dripped down onto my suit.

It wasn't as hot as before, but it was after midnight, so I undid my tie and unbuttoned my collar and looked up to see that everyone had turned into white-feather-headed vultures, their white shirts collared under black ties, their black suits and black dresses too, their champagne flutes in their hands. I saw the one with horn-rimmed glasses going around with a bottle of champagne to fill up their glasses as they held them up to each other in threes and fours, though I couldn't hear what they toasted to because they talked to each other like they were speaking in tongues. When the one with horn-rimmed glasses saw me, he came over to offer me some and I drank it straight from the bottle and it was good.

I'm starting to see things.

What things.

Things the way they are.

Is that good or bad.

I don't think so.

He frowned.

Did I ever tell you about the buzzards and the bees. Everyone here is here for my funeral. I'm sick of the buzzards in their white feathers and black suits.

Maybe you should have a drink. You don't look too good.

I drank some more of the champagne and it tasted like nothing and tasted like water. Well, for the time being we're immortal but we're so post-apocalyptic we're pre-apocalyptic. The real madness isn't in moments of seeing things that might not be there, but in realizing there's nothing else to see but what is there. I closed an eye then the other then both then I opened them again only to see they were all still where they were. Do you have anything to bring me back from the dead.

Yeah.

There are these things that either speed up or slow down one's own madness. I need those, not the other sorts of things that introduce a new madness to one's mind. The mind is the mouth of madness and my mouth is too full to swallow.

He laughed and handed me two pills. Take two and see where they take you.

Ignorance is God. Lo and behold. I drank the pills down. What did you give me.

A good time.

I think I need some air.

He agreed and I gave him back his bottle and left to go outside but at the sliding door saw my reflection and there were two horns like two branches growing out of my head and I said, You're each your own antler but the horns are coming out of my head. On the other side of the door was myself with the head of a snake. He stuck his forked tongue out and we reached for the handle to open the door as my horned reflection disappeared. There was only the serpent and he said to me, I is God.

I is God.

I is God, yes.

Coming up from behind him was a woman in black with the head of a panther. She had something of a sparkler in her hand. I turned to see if the vultures were seeing what was going on then I fainted when I saw standing before me only the panther-headed woman with round yellow eyes and black slits for pupils staring at me.

Wake up nada. There was nothing for a second then there was a pain in my side with the smell of vomit coming down through my nostrils. I opened my eyes and could see Adam much taller than me, forcing his heel into my rib. It was dark where we were and I was on my side on the ground, but there was his childish face smiling and he crouched down and slapped me. Wake up, he said. We gotta get outta here.

Someone else said something I couldn't quite hear other than a sharp *s* that was loud.

It was too early to care what time it was. I sat up to breathe and coughed hard then wiped my mouth on my sleeve where there were crusted bits of red I hadn't washed off from last night, my mouth sore from opening too much for itself, but everything else didn't feel bad.

Adam helped me up and I saw there was Serrano in his underwear again and curled up in his bed against a redhead I couldn't recognize with her hair on her face. I started over to her to brush her hair back when Adam grabbed my shoulder and shook his head no then to the side to go, so I followed him out of the room, passing three others on the floor at the other side of the bed, all of them still dressed but sleeping close together and I didn't bother to see who they were.

When we were outside the room I closed the door behind me, following Adam downstairs and feeling my jaw and how swollen it felt that I wished I had something to drink to not feel it as much. We got to the bottom steps and Adam started straight ahead to leave, but then I stopped him with a hand on the door.

You want a beer, I asked.

There isn't any time.

There's never any time, there's never any time not to.

Fine, fuck.

Wait give me another pill.

Right now, why.

I feel like shit.

You drank a lot.

That's not bothering me. I think I might've done something bad.

What'd you do.

I can't remember what it was. I can feel the pain to kill though.

He sighed and reached into his jacket for the bottle then he told me, You need to take better care of yourself.

I'm not myself.

No one else is.

This is the first time I've slept all year.

What.

I hadn't slept in three days, I said staring at the bottle in his hands. Always leave one for the morning, though. The golden rule.

Yeah yeah. He gave me one of the pills and said, We'll bring the car around.

Just one, I asked. The one in the morning is a metaphorical one. It means more than one. Give me another one.

I'll give you the second one when you get the fuck outside.

I laughed since there was nothing else for me to do. If you want to forget about something bad you've done, do something worse. I swallowed the pill dry and frowned then opened the door for Adam and saluted him as he walked down the driveway into the dawn.

I wasn't hungover, but I coughed again. My collar was undone, so I did it and buttoned up my jacket, brushing at the footprint of dust on my side I couldn't get rid of it all. I tiptoed down the hallway into the emptied kitchen, my footsteps all I heard walking up to the screen door that was closed all the way, though I could see some of the early morning through the mesh and I slid the door open slowly just wide enough for me to get through without it screeching too much.

The backyard smelled like the dried vomit and blood still

in my nose and felt like it should be colder than it was. The partygoers who never made it home last night never made it inside either. They would have looked like corpses if their chests weren't moving up and down or if they didn't shift their weight back and forth from time to time like they were dying. I headed for the bar as I passed the ones at the patio asleep on the sofas and I went to the bucket at its side where the beer bottles had been left in ice water overnight. I stuck my hands into the bucket and took two in each that were just as cold in the morning. I fit three of the bottles into my jacket pockets then opened one with the top pressed against the edge of the bar table, hitting it with my fist a few times until it opened as if it had been shaken, the head spilling off around the sides, so I held it to my mouth. It was good to drink and I grabbed two more beers, having half of the one I opened by the time I got to the driveway and Adam still wasn't there. I finished my beer and left it in the gutter with a handful of other cups and I opened up a second one against a third.

A long, black American Dream of a car, its windows rolled down, Adam, half his body outside the passenger window, pulled up a few feet in front of me and slowed to a stop a few feet past me and honked its horn.

Your chariot awaits, Adam said then he smiled his swollen cheeked smile and sat in again.

It looked like it had a few more payments left, how bright it contrasted with everything else in the street in the morning. I went to open the car door and it looked filled as I emptied my pockets into their hands and forced myself into the back where there were four of us.

New year new beer, the redhead at the other end said.

Does anyone have a lighter, the one in the middle of the three of them asked.

Or a bottle opener, the redhead said.

They were all a no and I was too, going through my pockets until I felt a pack of cigarettes inside my jacket and a white lighter I handed to them. The brunette next to me with her leg against mine and a seam in her stocking hadn't gotten a beer, so I offered her some of mine, but she held her hand to her mouth and might have been drunk still.

It's gonna be okay dear, another day another year.

She didn't say anything.

Do you know where we're going.

No.

Do you know where you're going. Adam and I just dodged the draft you know. The beach, no, not for us, we're a couple of deserters.

She had nothing to say.

Long days make for short nights. Or is it, long nights make for short days.

The lighter was passed back to me then the bottles too and I opened them out the window one at a time until they stopped foaming, the wind cold as fast as we were going, but the sun warm. I wondered where we were headed, but then I just drank as Adam shared his with the brunette who was driving. I tried from time to time with the one with her leg close to mine, but she was drunk, not a good one either, all the better as it was in drinking not to be a good drinker but to be a good drunk, so I drank for both of us since she might have vomited if she drank, the way some of them vomited at the smell of vomit, which I must have smelled bad to her because of the vomit.

I sat forward and shook Adam by the shoulder for him to say something.

He couldn't hear me over the wind and I leaned in closer and told him, I don't think I'm up for it today.

What.

I think I might be suffering from pretraumatic stress disorder.

Yeah me too.

He didn't know what he was talking about, but it was nice

for him to act like he did. I sat back into the seat and drank. I stared down at the legs of the one next to me, but she didn't cross them. I looked up at her from the side, the glitter around her blue eyes, which must have been red from not going to bed. Adam turned around to face us and without saying anything opened and closed his mouth several times to feel his jaw. He still looked like a child.

Are you going to the party tonight, the one in between asked him.

If everyone else is gonna be there.

I doubt that, but you should go.

Yeah you should come.

I thought we were going to South America to look for the tree of life, I said.

South America sounds nice this time of year, the redhead said.

We'd be looking for gold, Adam said. Which I know where it is.

Sounds good, the redhead said. Where is it.

In the ground.

Sounds gold, she said.

I couldn't remember her name but knew it was a good one that started with a *d* and finished in an open-ended vowel deep down in the throat to suspend the name there like Diana or Deanna or Deandra. I mouthed her names and remembered speaking to her several times in a few years but remembered nothing she or I had said, though I knew she had a good name, but knowing people only in passing at parties it was always too late to ask anyone their name again.

The brunette leaned her head back and closed her eyes then leaned her head on the one sitting in the middle. She sat forward and the brunette leaned her head back again.

Are you two gonna go to the funeral for Andrea, the one in the middle asked Adam and me.

When is it again, Adam asked.

I don't remember, she said and she looked at me.

I don't know, I said. I don't think so. I didn't know her that well.

Yeah, it's too bad.

Diana or Deanna or Deandra asked, So you're going to the party instead of Southern America.

Adam tugged at his neckbeard and thin goatee. He looked like a conquistador. Jess, para ti too night, jess. Después de Baja America.

They all laughed as Diana or Deanna or Deandra blushed, roundfaced with the sort of Eastern European face some half of the world found attractive, though I never really got into as much, the color leaving her face when the rest of them were finished with their fits. Antes, she said.

Jess, the Andes. Jess.

The brunette leaned her head forward and looked around.

I asked her again, Do you know where we're going.

No, she said and she closed her eyes.

The rest of the ride was quiet because we didn't want to waste whatever we had to say to them when we saw them that night and because the wind covered most of what we said. I sat back and drank as Adam gave directions to where he was staying with his mother for the winter and when we got there Adam hugged the brunette who drove us and said he would see her tonight then we got out and stood in the driveway to wave them off and watch them turn the corner, staying there as they drove back around and went the other way down to the main street. We waved until they were gone again.

Hold on a second, Adam whispered. I'll be right back. He then went up the driveway past two foreign-made sedans of the same model, a newer black one and an old beige one, the black more rounded than the angled beige.

The buzz had left a bad taste in my mouth. I tried to retighten my tie, but I couldn't get it right without looking in a mirror. It was bright as day for morning. There was a faded white line in the sky, whatever had made it gone. It looked like there was dew in the grass, but the blades stood up straight to their ends.

Adam shook the keys softly and motioned me over to the beige sedan. He left it in neutral and I pushed it out of the driveway and into the street some, but it wasn't too bad with the bit of slope down the length of the drive. I got in and Adam wrestled with the wheel and the engine struggled to turn over, but when it did he made a show of going backwards down to the end of the street and reversing into the wider but also empty main street.

It smells like my father, he said with his hand shaking the stick shift.

It didn't smell like anything to me, so I didn't say anything.

I'm hungry.

I could eat.

We idled in the street and I was tired and closed my eyes for a while before the windows were rolled down and I felt the wind cold on my skin as we took off down the street. Adam drove most of the way slowly and I kept my eyes closed and stared at white dots until we stopped and it was a railroad crossing, the striped barriers swinging down as the red lights flashed and we heard the train coming across in front of us.

We should take the train to South America, I said.

No money.

You don't have any money.

I don't have any money.

No one has money.

You have more money than me.

It's not my money.

And I don't wanna go to South America.

Why's that.

I don't wanna die.

Why not.

All the drugs there. All the drugs you need are in your

head, your dopamines, your seratonics.

Yeah, but they make you drool from the mouth for all the wrong reasons.

What are the right reasons.

A good woman.

A good woman isn't hard to find.

Meeting someone and marrying her before you fall out of love though.

Adam shrugged and we watched the train going to the left.

Why don't we go up north for the weekend, I asked.

I was thinking we could head east for a while.

That's fine too, we could head north then come back around.

I'm sure we could do that, but why north.

There's lots of women and drugs I know up there.

Right.

I'll try to arrange something.

Adam just tugged at his neckbeard.

It's odd to stare at just the horizontal of the train, perpendicular. The train was mostly cargo. It isn't how it's supposed to be seen. It should be parallel, looking at the length of it.

What was up with you last night, he asked me.

Why, what happened.

You were chewing on your hand and saying it was the best apple you'd ever tasted.

I laughed and I told him, I don't remember that. Things sort of got out of hand.

The train passed us and I closed my eyes until we were pulling into one of those sort of diners that were still open since being a drive-in in the fifties, the lot still lined with cars, though we had to get out to go in and I felt out of place and buttoned up my jacket through the two sets of doors, surrounded by aluminum and neon, we belonged there in our suits. It was crowded so we walked down the aisle toward the end to seat ourselves closer to the street side window. I unbuttoned my jacket and sat down in the booth and Adam went through one of the slim menus left on the paper place setting. Most of them in the diner were too old to tell how early it was for them to be there. They took their time eating and I couldn't hear what they said, but they weren't saying much. The younger ones who seemed to have been out all night talked loudly like no one might hear them. I couldn't make sense of what they said with their mouths full, but their eyes were wild.

It's all lines in here.

Adam read his menu and didn't say anything.

Lines of lines.

He told me yesterday when we were walking up and down the aisles in a supermarket with no money to buy anything but a half an hour to kill, Everything in here's arranged into lines of lines. The diner was all lines too.

America is somewhere between a diner and a supermarket. A supermarket in the middle of the day and a diner in the middle of the night. The American Insomnia is to end the night under some halogen lighting that brings in the same woman in red and the man all in white and the man all in black. I was sure I knew what brought in the mothy sort to the nausea of hangover lighting.

The waitress came by and wasn't much to look at. I wasn't hungry but the coffee smelled good to me. She wore a white and pink uniform like she had once wished for immortality but forgot to ask about eternal youth. What can I get you two, she said and smiled at Adam to start.

I'll have the lumberjack special, eggs over easy, wheat toast, an orange juice and coffee please and thank you. Adam squinted to read her name tag and said, Anne. Thank you, Anne.

She smiled and turned to me.

I'll just have coffee.

You sure you don't want anything, she asked me.

You should get something.

Oh no, I looked at her name tag and saw she spelled it Ann. Thank you though, Ann.

You sure.

It's on me, Adam said.

No, really. I'm okay.

Rough night, Adam said to the waitress.

I'm trying to keep it from turning into a rough morning.

Adam shrugged at the waitress. He looked too young and acted too old for his age, which only endeared him to any woman over a certain age. She smiled and said she would be right back with our coffees. He watched her go to the booth at the end of our aisle to have the same conversation.

I really wanna fuck her in the ass.

Who, Ann. Maybe when she comes back. I think she's into you.

She looks like, what's her name, the one with the big ass she could barely fit in between our desks. I really wanted to fuck her in the ass every time she walked by.

Yeah. I think she was into you.

She knew what she was doing. She was straightening our desks.

Straightening our dicks.

The coffee came and it was all I could ask for, warm and settling in my stomach, it didn't feel as bad as before and I drank it black. Adam emptied a shot of cream and some sugar into his and let it sit for a while. I sank into the booth and held the mug against my stomach and felt good.

This place is both what they thought the past was like but wasn't and what the past thought the future would be like but isn't.

Yeah it's neither. But it's nice to have your picture up in places where they put up pictures. Let me ask you something. Isn't it weird that they have the same actors playing different roles, it's the same person right, this person's got the same face, he always looks the same. How am I supposed to believe he's someone else when he's always himself.

Adam's breakfast came and he thanked the waitress and she thanked him. He didn't watch her walk away this time but instead he covered his plate in maple syrup, softening it enough to chew slowly with mouthfuls of orange juice. Adam didn't like to talk about acting much, so he ate and I tried eavesdropping on some of the others across the aisle, but all they did was eat.

So what're you thinking we do.

About what.

Adam sipped his coffee and said, Getting outta here and going somewhere for a while.

I wouldn't mind going to the high deserts or mountain ranges or something. You know what. I think somewhere with trees, any sort of wilderness is fine with me. Why what were you thinking.

He ate for a while before he gave up and said, Fuck this hurts. He held his jaw and pushed the plate across the table. Have some of this.

I'm not hungry.

I can't eat it.

Why don't you take some of the oxycodone.

I need the money.

The egg yolk and syrup had swirled together, matting down the strips of bacon and half a pancake and slices of toast he had left me. Everything fell apart with the fork, so I left the knife dripping on the place setting. The ketchup and maple syrup had mixed together and tasted good.

Do you still talk to Amy, he asked me.

Not after the last time.

When was that.

I don't remember. I don't know, do you still talk to her.

I don't know. It was going good for a while. I think it was

one of the best things that happened to me. She paid for everything near the end, but it's one of those things, that if it lasted for twenty years it would have turned to shit. Then again I think she would make a great mother. But I really can't afford to be with her right now.

Yeah. You just have to find the one you don't want to just fuck in the ass.

He was better without her. I told him that more than once after she started going down on me. We all knew he knew, though it's not like I wouldn't have done it if I wasn't drunk or if she wasn't pretty or if she wasn't both, but it happened a few times altogether, so it wasn't that I was drunk a first time or didn't have to be drunk the next time, but it didn't matter in the end because the only reason they lasted as long as they did was they held on to each other closer afterwards. I had given them that.

She comes from people that aren't just rich but have been rich for a long time.

Yeah, they're not people anymore. Bloodlines, you know. Blood money. It's all lines.

He offered me the leftover orange juice, but I put my hand up and shook my head no with my mouth full. I swallowed then asked him, Still wanna go tonight though.

The beach.

The co-op.

Yeah why not.

Yeah, why not.

Need to make some money though.

Right.

Do you still have access to the library in Berkeley.

Yeah.

They've got a big collection there too don't they.

I think it's the largest in the country.

And you can still check out books from there.

Yeah.

Then we can go up there for a while, there's wilderness there, we make some money or maybe we even get some temporary work to fuel the trip, something legitimate maybe as lumberjacks or longshoremen, something like that.

So what's it about the library.

What you do is you check out first editions of library books, sell them for the several hundred they're worth, then when you report the book stolen to the library and they fine you or ask you to replace it, you replace it with a second edition, just as old but only worth a few bucks.

I laughed.

I was making a profit doing it in New York until I got arrested and what not. I couldn't check out anymore books to pay for the ones that were that became overdue, then if I reported them as being lost, I would have to pay the fines, which I didn't have enough money to, then at the same time each of the overdue books was being added to a dollar a day until the waiting period ended and they were just categorized as lost either way. All these systems have checks and balances to prevent people like us from ever getting away with too much.

Some idiots probably requested the books back early so they could write their term papers.

Yeah, probably the same motherfucks who throw themselves off the top floor of the library to kill themselves. You know, they painted this optical illusion sort of thing on the ground floor to make it look like spikes, so they don't jump, cause looking down it looks like you'll be impaled.

Death will stop most people from committing suicide.

Ann came back with the check and left it face down on the table, Whenever you're ready.

Adam stopped her. I'm sorry, I didn't see it on the menu, but do you have any smoothies.

No, we do have milkshakes. She turned the menu over to its back.

Oh, that's okay then. He sighed. Thank you though.

I'm sorry.

She turned to go, but he stopped her again. He asked, Could I just get a cup of ice actually.

Of course.

He waited for her to leave then dry heaved as he said, Milkshakes. He shuddered. Cows make cows out of people.

Yeah, I looked at all the others in the diner. The cattle. Where can we get a car.

We can use mine. My mother would still want a couple hundred for it.

Do you have a couple hundred.

We'll go halves on it.

Do you have half a couple hundred.

Not on me, no.

The old beige sedan he needed several hundred for had belonged to his father then to him before he asked his mother for several hundred for it, which he sold to pay several thousand dollars and all of his inheritance to a lawyer. I told him, I don't wanna buy you a car.

You'll be buying yourself a car. You'll be a car owner, nada. And we'll be sleeping in the car at times too, so you'll practically be a homeowner.

I don't drive.

Since when.

Since never, I'm never driving again. So there's no point in me owning a car.

What if I were to sell the rest of the pills to you wholesale, three each instead of four.

No, give them to me with the money for the rest of them too.

I don't have it anymore.

Why not.

I invested it already.

In what.

A business.

What business.

None of your business. Adam tugged at his neckbeard as the waitress came by with the coffee pot and I slid my cup to the edge of the table, which she filled to the brim and I thanked her. She moved to pour for Adam, but he covered his cup with his hand and thanked her as she left. Well, if you want to know, I think I might be headed to Florida. I've been speaking with this man there who's been working on a machine that produces matter. I don't want to go into it now, I'd have to give you some of the literature on it to read. We've been in correspondence for a while now but I think all we need is some investors for him to finish building what he's been working on.

Why're you always plotting shit. Just do something good instead of all these stupid little plots.

Adam laughed. On the way there we could do whatever, stop by everything on the way.

I shrugged. As long as we're headed east, right. I'm alright with something cross country.

Good.

But I'll try to arrange some things up north.

I don't know if that's a good idea. I say we just show up. I wanna be those two guys that show up wearing suits, and for a week everyone'll be asking who the fuck are those two guys.

Women and drugs, we're gonna do a lot of them.

I don't know about the drugs.

But the women.

And I'll throw in the rest of the prescription as well, he said and he rattled the bottle of pills.

Let me see them. I opened the bottle and took two with the orange juice.

Why don't you hold onto them.

Yeah, thanks. I opened the bottle again and looked inside. It's half empty.

You had half of it when it was full.

I was too tired to count, so I didn't say anything.

Let's get all our things together then, tonight we pick up and head north.

Pack up and pick up.

And really we wouldn't have to give my mother the money until the end of the week.

I don't give a motherfuck.

Adam looked at the check and put it face down again and stared out the window. It's too fucking hot in this city to smoke a cigarette. Now New York is a city that pairs well with a cigarette. I think it's good we're heading east. He slid the check over to me and said, You did have most of it.

You motherfuck.

I don't have any money on me nada. And you owe me for the rest of the pills right now, and I was the one that got us the car, which was my inheritance. I'll pay you back once we get up to Berkeley. I also will have a lot more once we get to Florida. Adam always smiled when he was serious and he was smiling then.

Yeah, yeah. Fuck you.

The lawyer had proved that Adam had a history of mental instability, maybe just by saying he had paid several thousand dollars and all of his inheritance to prove he was mentally instable, but one would have to be mad not to go crazy, because it didn't even come close to the debt he had left over from three years of acting school before he finished without a degree.

Adam stood up to go and I left the money on the table and tipped well enough to want to fuck Ann in the ass.

I looked worse than the night before but better than the morning after in the evening when Adam showed up in the beige sedan I doubted could make it across the country or up north or even into the city. He honked the horn, got out to open the trunk then got back inside and reversed then hit the brakes hard to close the trunk only to get out to open it again. He had his clothes folded with some odds and ends in one half of the trunk, so I left my bags in the other half. It didn't look like it would turn out to be much of a trip because we didn't have much, but Adam pulled out a bottle of whiskey he said he found in the trunk, so we had some then put it back.

It was sort of cold for such a warm Los Angeles winter, but Adam rolled down his window as we started for the co-op, nearing the end of a purple sunset from the smog from the highway when I asked to pull over before we got on, so I could get the bottle of whiskey and not waste the onset of another pair of pills, getting back in and opening the dashboard to find a Bible in there I put the bottle on top of then asked Adam about it.

It's a bestseller, he said as we got on the highway.

It was hard to tell which way we were going until the evening darkened some then all the cars up ahead flickered their lights on, in a few minutes the whole highway lit white and red. The city was wide enough to always be going somewhere into the city and coming from somewhere in the city and going to somewhere else in the city. It was the time of night to go into the city, but soon enough everything would be turned up too bright to see anything else.

Adam drove back and forth across all the lanes like his father had never allowed him to drive when he was a child. He would say something and I would nod my head and agree with him. He pressed the car with the windows rolled up and all the electronics turned off, all the power pushed forward to the motor, which rattled past sixty until there was a whirring sound that came from the front right wheel like it was about to tear apart, but then it screeched into a high-pitched hum as we reached eighty, the sound finally disappearing as the windows struggled to hold back the wind through their seals.

I sank into my seat and waited for the warmth and drank some then everything started to slow down and after a while we weren't moving at all but instead lurching forward from time to time. Adam started the radio and we listened for too long to the static coming through the mountains. I could tell the car shuddered with the same delirium tremens we were in, starting and stopping the same as the car before us and after, but then the radio came through and settled in with a stranger sound, the sound of trumpets and a piano stretched across the chest, the sound of mariachi music. The horns deceived how slow we were passing the scene with several sirens going and the lights signaling some accident up ahead. I stared at the white and red of the sirens and I watched all the others with their heads turned hoping to see something good and I stuck my head out the window and yelled over the mariachi music, Fuck you fucks.

Ai yai yai yai.

Motherfucks.

Ai yai yai yai yai.

Sometimes the static took over but Adam still twirled like a mariachi, speaking in tongues, his swollen jaw left untreated for too long, but there was the bottle in the dashboard and the bottle in my pocket. I read the name on the prescription and it was his. I prepared both of the bottles. The anesthetic would have to fill in for the synesthetic.

I think what we're suffering from here is some sort of self-misdiagnosis.

He was eager to get going again.

Take two and see where they take you.

There's three there.

Right, I said and I took two of them. I'll be the control.

I'm gonna try to take the exit up here.

I held my hand out again and told him, One and done.

He took the pill without the whiskey and still I hoped it would bring him to his senses, but we would have to wait and see what happened. I could see he was in no condition to drive, but I was too afraid to worry him with the truth. He had turned the car and merged his way across the lanes until he had turned us sideways, pulling onto the shoulder and for a second we saw the city, there wasn't a skyline but all the lights in one flat line, the sounds of the horns over everything else.

We were making good time again, for Adam never having been to the co-op before, but I tried to think of giving him directions from memory, only knowing it would come back to me once we were a little west of West Hollywood and I could tell him his lefts from his rights.

We were no worse for wear after circling around the co-op several times until we settled for leaving the car at the end of some side street. The walk wasn't bad, breathing in the breeze coming off of the ocean, though the ocean must have been more than a few miles away. I was unsure which way we were headed, uphill and downhill a few times over with the street winding back and forth, but when we turned the corner so did the corner after it and the one after that. The dry wind that always comes from the mountains and blows the dust in the city from fall into winter had died down for the night, most of the trees left bare and a few branchless when the leaves came and left like locusts.

I think I'm suffering from some neurosis of the liver.

That doesn't sound too bad.

I can't remember the last time I had something to drink.

I have to piss.

I'm not sure if I have to or if I do, but the oxycodone must be wearing off.

I haven't felt anything.

You're not supposed to feel anything.

Adam shrugged.

I told him, I feel nothing.

Is that good.

No, I'm feeling pretty prenostalgic.

Adam walked ahead like he knew where we were going, but the way the streets curved toward each other we might have ended up where we were again, so he just went to piss on a tree. Drinking was always looking for a place to piss. I went on without him slowly since it was a party that didn't matter if we didn't get there on time. The houses didn't look the same like they were stopped in their tracts or like they were built one after the other, but rather one not after the other, some tall apartments in between them, hard to tell which one was which when they were so different, but the co-op was on one of the corners around there. Adam caught up to me and it was a quiet night except for the two of us being there, lights clicking on from Adam setting off sensors and stepping in and out of the sidewalk and into driveways and lawns.

Do you remember when we were running down one of these streets, maybe this one. We were in our underwear and there were those girls in the pool waiting for us. When was that, that was a long time ago. Then those security guards came in the middle of the night and dragged us out.

My grandfather told me how when he was young he saw these two guys who were on opium, they were looking down at this puddle in front of their feet asking where they could get a boat to get across the ocean.

I don't remember that.

There was something up ahead and we went over and walked in the street and listened and we went toward it until we started to see the same cars on the sides of the street.

I had lost Adam when I went to find something to drink, but there was everyone else again. They sounded the same as last night but off-pitch and they looked more like each other in the same but dulled brown attire that made them look less like themselves. They were taking their time turning their cigarettes into ashes and butts, the atrium in the middle of the co-op littered with them, slow to drink the champagne that looked thoroughly decanted, though not on the right end of midnight but rather waiting for midnight like it wouldn't come.

The night was slow poured into champagne flutes, but Adam and I had agreed to leave before this one died down the way last night did. I held my flute upside down to my lips to get a last bit, but the foam sat on the sides fermenting and the rest must have evaporated because nothing came down to the mouthpiece. I would have gone straight to the bar to get more if they weren't taking turns filling up flutes, the ones pouring for me the last time telling me it was leftover champagne that had flattened out from several parties last night. It's a sham champagne, one of them said. It is isn't it, I asked him then smiled a laugh to drink one then take another and tell him I thought it was called champagne because it didn't cause a hangover. The flute felt smaller in my hand once it was empty. I watched the ones in line to get drunk and wasn't sure that they weren't always so dull brown, that it wasn't always so hard to tell who was who. I repeated, It's a *sham*pagne.

Hey stranger.

Audra stared up at me, her dull brown hair and eyebrows, never where I left her, always with the dimple on the one cheek. She said something else but I couldn't hear her over all of the music that wasn't supposed to be heard as much as it was felt hard in the lungs.

Hey yourself. I exhaled smoke and saw the half-cigarette left between my fingers that couldn't have been mine if it hadn't been lit and left there for me to hold to my mouth while I thought of something to say her. I asked her, Do you want the rest of this.

She smiled and I held the end to her mouth and she inhaled and exhaled, mouthing something for me to nod and look at everyone else. If anyone didn't know anyone there, though they all did, the co-op was known as the international house, most of them having had expatriated an hour or less from home, not that there weren't others that had come a long way to end up in the co-op.

Yeah I can never finish one of these, I told her. I'm more of a drag queen.

Okay, your highness. She smiled and took the cigarette from me and she drank some from her flute, making a face as she held it up to me. Wouldn't you think that champagne that's been aged for another year would taste better. She drank again then scratched her tongue with her teeth and handed me her champagne to drink. Not a bestseller.

I know what you mean. All we can do is stand around drinking the same shit and repeating the same. My hearing had gone all of a sudden like someone had put their fingertips in my ears. Shit. I could see her nodding for me to finish. The same shit to each other. My voice came out clear in my head and resounded in some cranial cavity like it had nowhere else to go but bounce around a while in my mind before it spilled out as slow as she nodded, taking her time to hold the cigarette to her mouth. There was only my voice and a faint ringing in my head and I tugged at my earlobe and flattened my ear, opening and closing my mouth to force myself to swallow air.

Audra said something and I leaned in as close as I could for her to whisper into my ear so no one could hear her, every *s* pronounced soft but sharp, hissing into my head. Trying to say something clever, she said. She was brightly colored in her beige dress and she stuck out against all of the matching brown coats and brown dresses. Or insightful. They were all in on it, but they didn't know what it was. Or clever.

I laughed and could hear her better, so I laughed again.

I'm so fucking bored with everything everyone's ever said.

Everyone's fucked everyone here.

Not everyone.

I laughed.

We never did go all the way.

I'm attracted to older women but all the girls I end up with are much younger than me.

I'm not younger than you, you know that right.

You're such a contrarian.

Am I.

Yeah, even there the go-to line would've been, no I'm not, but you refused to do that too.

She laughed then took her time smoking the half-cigarette, everything slowing down again as they all cremated themselves from the inside out on their stale cigarettes and champagne in turn-of-the-century clothes, still unsure of which century it was, the halfs and the half-nots. They were stripped film that I could see them, drab and dull, faceless brownian creatures, the most troubling thing to each of them being that there might be nothing at all wrong with them. I could see them all colorless and blind.

Tell me something, she said.

Right, what would you like to hear, dear. Let's see, where do I begin.

Shush. She covered my mouth with her hand, tapping her fingers on my cheek, which I could feel were warm and I tried to smell but couldn't, licking her palm and tasting nothing. The senses were starting to go as she shushed everything in my head. You talk too much, she said. Her hand crawled up to the top of my head and her fingers through my hair and she held it there. You think too much too.

You're much too much. I interlocked fingers with her,

pulled her hand off my head and putting it on the side of hers pushed it through her shorter hairs to the top of her head. She squinted at me and I ran her hand through her hair and scratched the top of her head. What do you think.

Do you want to do some nitrous oxide.

I moved her hand back to the top of my head to make it scratch my scalp then nod, Yes. Much too much, lead the way.

Audra led me by the fingertips as things took a turn again, the film wearing thin on everyone and everything dimming, the champagne the end of me, though I wasn't sure where it went. I had lost most control of my limbs and would have fallen over if she wasn't holding my hand. It was a bluish brown mess of bodies that slowly blackened as my head spun and I was pulled forward.

Hey stranger.

Can I have a drag, I asked her and she held the end of the cigarette to my lips for me to suck it out from between her fingers like it was one of her breasts before she pulled it away from me and I let go of the smoke through my nose. I made a fist and coughed into it and I felt my throat but it didn't feel bad to breathe hard. What am I supposed to feel like. I could see a bit better the more I said to her, though they all looked the same and we had only moved to the other end of the crowd since she had held my hand. Everyone faded into outlines and their mouths moved but they didn't speak. The waiting was familiar to them. Like, what's it supposed to do. She stood in frame again while everything else faded into some chiaroscuro.

Are you talking too much again.

I don't know. How will I know when I'm feeling the nitrous oxide.

You haven't done it yet.

Right, it hasn't kicked in yet.

No we haven't done it at all.

Yeah I don't feel anything. It's not very good nitrous

oxide. Let me ask you something though, let's say it was, what would I feel.

I think the idea is that it's better not to, but if I had to.

Yes you have to.

I'd say it feels a little like a mild euphoria.

That sounds kinda good.

It does, doesn't it.

She turned her back to me and disappeared.

Adam had told me how he met one of the international women from the co-op the other night and fell for her the moment he saw her, but she said how it was her last semester before she had to go back to her country, though he found out at the end of the night that she was faking her accent to mess with him, which I tried to tell him was good because it meant she must not have been going back to her country and he could see her after all, but he was too heartbroken to be bothered. Maybe he went to go look for her though.

Everyone's fucked over everyone here, I said to someone.

She turned to me again with a brown balloon in her hand. The waiting had slowed everything, but she held the end of the balloon toward my mouth and I leaned in to feel the bit of rubber and she smiled then opened her fingers against my lips for me to inhale and as I did the air rushed in and my cheeks swelled until she tore the balloon away to cover my lips under her palm, so I held my breath and I felt alive again, tasting the only air in the atrium, watching her shrink the balloon into her mouth.

She couldn't hear me so I winked at her and exhaled into her hand to say something, but again she held the balloon up to my mouth. There was no reason not to. The dull brown wore off when I breathed in again and I could see them, still bluish brown but better than before, laughing and I felt good to see them. There was a celluloid jump when I exhaled and again I inhaled the balloon and everything shrank into an iris, the camera obscura, again I exhaled and the balloon was there again as I watched their cigarettes burning up like when they first started smoking cigarettes and they smoked them too quickly, lit up like the sparklers at midnight while they had all turned into a phantasmagoria of firebreathers lighting their cigarettes end to end to breathe up all the air they turned into ashes falling down from their mouths. There was another skip in the celluloid and the balloon was there again and she was too, photogenic in such a small aperture, a starlet of a black and white and silent screen, eyes swimming in the white spots, looking for some light to focus, a flashbulb went off and she held the balloon to her mouth again, her cheeks filled the way she had fit most of me inside them. I tried to kiss them down as she exhaled and I could see her sucking it all in again and again.

How do you feel.

I think I'm suffering from some mild euphoria.

That's nothing to suffer.

I feel like a child. Something about the balloons.

Suffer the children.

Nostalgic oxide.

She held a hand on my chest and pushed down the leftover breath and it was done. The atrium was as small as the first time I had really seen it, some of them were there with balloons, some of them with their cigarettes.

Do you wanna take some inside and dance.

Yes. I mean, yes. I rather would much rather.

She went to stand in line where there were several of them who weren't dressed like everyone else and looked like they had just heard the music and came in to try to give the international one with horn-rimmed glasses and the nitrous oxide tank a handful of dollars for several balloons, but he said in some accent that there weren't any balloons left. She passed them to fill ours again and when she came back she pushed me through the crowd to go inside, handing me the balloon that I inhaled from. I sank back enough into my eyes to not see where we were going, the music loud and heavy on the heart, but it was the leftover champagne that had done me in. She pushed me in and I heard the music then I heard nothing, but then again I heard the music then again nothing, on and on, on and off, off and on, alternating it and nothing, no, not nothing, no, nothingness.

We were headed straight into the middle of them, crowded as it was there as it was outside but closer together and they were trying harder to touch each other in the dark. It was hard to breathe without the balloon, moving through them and trying to hold onto Audra, my peripherals fading again, I held onto the balloon tighter and bent my back and overarched my spine backwards to try see more in front of me. There was no difference between them how close they were then, inside and out the same faceless faces, black-figured outside as they were red-figured inside, wet with each other's sweat, beasts with one back between them. We were in the middle of it all and she pulled me back to face her then turned around and pushed herself up against me to dance the way all of them did, the jitterbuggery, everyone in one mass to some tantric end. Things were quick to take a turn for the bacchanalian and I couldn't tell if it was in the one good or one of the many bad ways, but foresight is always fifty-fifty. They had come in on an upbeat without knowing what the measure was, so the way it was, measures would have to be taken, as good a time as it was to sink down into myself and fall under the tranquility of the pills, the certainty of their dosage. They moved up and down with each other even when there was nothing to move to and the music had ended and I was left the colorblind cyclops among the colorless and blind.

Audra turned around with her hand outstretched and we took two pills together with the rest of the balloon and we waited, but the music started up again and she turned around and I felt her in front of me, her ass against me. She turned to face me again and put her thigh between my legs and mouthed something, putting her hand down my pants and pulling on my dick then sticking a fingernail inside to a sharp sting at the tip that I backed away from as she pulled her hand out and on the back of my neck to lower my head to hers. Her eyes were blue when she smiled.

I want to stick my cock into your eyesocket.

She smiled.

And fuck your brains out.

She shook her head and pointed at her ear.

Until they come pouring out of your ears.

She said something and I went to her ear and asked her what she said and she did the same.

There isn't anything mild about it is there.

No, not at all.

She shrugged her shoulders and I turned her around and put a hand on her stomach to pull her against me while I bit her neck up to her earlobe. I breathed in and out of her ear and felt as good myself, putting a hand on her breast and another down her dress then up again before she pushed it away and bent over to disappear.

The light turned on and off then on again and I saw them all in seconds. I stood still and I was moved back and forth in the same suspended motion and my head spun and I looked for a way out with one eye closed then the other one. The whole world looked closer with one eye closed. My vision had faded from a bluish brown to a blackened and misshaped zero, but all my other senses were sharpened then and though they were no longer dimorphic I could tell them apart by the way they smelled and if they smelled bad, but the repeated wear of rubbing up against each other in their suits and dresses, the purgatorial sort of contractions, soon enough had them all smelling the same. They had to think that in hell it isn't the heat but the humidity that gets the most complaints. I looked down and saw her bent over and headless, half herself. We had to get out of there before it all came falling down.

I gotta get outta here, I told her and I turned to get out of there.

Something pushed up against me then turned my shoulder to pass through. I couldn't tell what it was but there was another behind it, so I held onto the second one and fell in line, soon enough something else putting a hand on my shoulder, though I couldn't make heads or tails of myself.

Where are we going.

The one behind me wasn't aware that we were going in circles.

Can you drop me off at the end of the crowd.

The one in front could only see where we were going in the seconds of light.

I think I'm suffering from solipsistic fibrosis.

The line had grown to consume the whole crowd.

I can't breathe. I think I might be dying or dead.

They said nothing because they were all holding their deaths in their mouths.

Solipsistic fibrosistic fibrosism.

The one in front of me stopped. I pressed on ahead of him and I saw how the one in front was caught up in a mass of them and already matching his hips with someone with several thrusts up and down and he was gone, but looking back I saw the rest of the line was lost to the crowd. The one behind me pushed me to the side and when the light hit his head I saw that it was the phrenological figurehead. I asked him if he knew which way was out, but he didn't hear me, so I followed him as he wandered ahead until he pressed up against someone, his eyes half-closed, champagne flute in the air, his eyes rolling back, unaware of anything that wasn't in front of him. Ignorance is God. Some of them had to have their eyes closed to not see who was in front of them and some of them had to have had their eyes open but didn't see who was behind them, but I was in between open and closed.

The closer to being blind, the better I could see what I saw, but then there was nothing.

I am no one.

Everything I knew was the tail end of oneself, the ringing heard at either end of everything, of the synesthetic life turned anesthetic, when one cannot taste and one cannot touch and one cannot know such truths when they are lost inside each other, when can one smell and when can one see and cannot help but hear how the small separation between the ears makes one to know one. One might be better off to purge oneself and let us begin again then, the internal being the eternal, the way in being the way out, but we bang and we whimper and all we can do is bang again.

I is God.

There was nothing and there was nothing to make sense of as I waded into the deep end and I was there because there was nothing there to tell the difference, to make heads or tails of myself, was I or was I not the serpent-tailed lion or the lion-headed serpent or the serpent-headed lion or the lion-tailed serpent. I breathed in to myself and breathed out to God.

Hallelujah Hare Krishna.

Krishna Krishna Hallelujah.

Hallelujah Hare Rama.

Rama Rama Hallelujah.

Everything came out of the iris again as a train coming through a tunnel and out the projection for me while I waited and breathed in and out again, it all falling into focus again out of the black and into the brown and I could see everything. There was another line of them and I followed the last one without asking which way they were headed until we reached the end of the room. I left it and went out to the balcony where it was cold and I saw the night and I could see Los Angeles.

They were all there too on the balcony, two persons thin

but a hundred or more of them long, talking between cigarettes and champagne, the ones with their backs to the city leaning against a concrete barrier, the ones standing against the wall of the co-op to look at each other and the light from the city. I was cold and I had sweated out everything I drank and felt sober. I took my jacket off and it was soaked, but I was cold and I put it back on.

Hey man do you know where that white girl is at, someone asked me.

White girl, I asked. Yeah, she's inside. Which one.

He stared at me then stretched out the word, Cocaine.

Oh sorry, I am soberingly drunk. I don't have any.

He laughed at me. Fuckin faggot.

I left him at the start of the balcony and started halfway to the end before I saw Adam talking to some blonde and I gave up on getting something else to drink.

We gotta get outta here man, I said.

When did we get here.

The blonde started talking to someone else.

Adam tried to shoulder into her other conversation then turned back to me, What time is it.

I don't know. Does it matter. We gotta get out while the getting is good.

He looked at the blonde and smiled at me. Fuck man, these girls are just girls. We turned to go and when we got to the end of the balcony he looked back and asked, Don't you just love getting high. He took a hit off a joint that wasn't there and passed it to me coughing and he laughed. It was louder being back inside as the strobe lights lit and unlit and I wondered where we would go and where the car was, thought of the engine having to turn over several times before we were to head east, feeling the same mild euphoria from before to take the joint from his hand and bring it in between my index and forefinger up to my mouth, but then there was nothing then everything then nothing again.

We went down Sunset Boulevard where it winded in between the rich estates with the long driveways we could almost see to their ends and the richer estates with hedges lining their yards so we couldn't see inside. There were palm trees planted on the sides of the street and bent toward each other like they were looking for water or like they were blowing in the wind. There was the whir from the wheel then the hum and we were in West Hollywood before we slowed down to the whir again and rolled our windows down as we hit traffic, Adam turning one way or the other if someone else turned left or right, halfway in each lane at all times, everyone else pulling out of the bars while everyone leftover for us was good and drunk.

He stuck his tongue out and didn't have to signal when he changed lanes or have to look in the mirror, spinning the wheel this way and that, struggling to steer us somewhere. I turned the radio on and spun through the static and the stations then turned it off. I sank back into my seat to keep rowing us forward, but then there was nothing left to do but take another pill since I had gone far enough in the deep end to know where I could play in the shallows.

Don't you want your window down.

What, I asked Adam. Yeah, sure. I sat up and rolled the window back down.

You were in a bad way back there.

Yeah. I think I needed to feel bad to figure out why we're trying so hard to feel good.

Started talking to people that weren't there.

That sounds like me. I laughed.

He didn't say anything, but maybe he didn't hear me.

That sounds like me. Thanks though.

Yeah.

I thought I saw some things, but then I thought that wouldn't it be more terrifying if there was something there I didn't see. I hope I didn't ruin your time though did I.

They were girls.

We can go back if you wanna go back. There are still a lot of girls there to fuck.

I don't want to fuck anyone you've already fucked.

I haven't fucked all of them.

Yeah, but someone there has.

There was a neon sign up ahead that read Girls Girls Girls and stuck out bright enough against the dark building below it that maybe it was the contrast that sold someone on turning right at the side street ahead or maybe it was getting out of the traffic that was enough, but maybe it was just that the pink neon read Girls Girls Girls.

Girls girls girls.

Girls, fuck. If we're still calling girls girls in a few years. If all girls are girls. Then all girls are girls. We should only be calling girls girls.

What, like little girls.

Yeah.

It wasn't late enough for the sign to be the last bit of light shining against the end of the night, but rather still early enough for us to search for somewhere where they weren't just girls.

Girls girls girls. It's like sex drugs and rock 'n' roll. Rock 'n' roll just means sex. It's sex, drugs, and sex. Sex, drugs, and sex. I don't know any more mass addictive drug than sex, so it really has to just be, sex sex and sex. But sex is the drug. One or the other, or one or the other, so girls girls girls are drugs drugs drugs.

Women and drugs, we're gonna do a lot of them, right.

Right.

I don't think you're ever gonna see a neon sign that says drugs drugs drugs.

Maybe not.

We started and stopped again and all the girls were behind us, though farther down and across the street was the Chateau Marmont and around it there were billboards with half-nude actresses, which covered up most of the hotel about as good as the thick hedges and taller palms below the billboards, the shorter palms like cypress shrubs along the street making it look like Alexandria.

Do you think you'd want to have children, I asked Adam.

Yeah, I don't see why not. We waited for some light up ahead to turn. There was a line of them across the street waiting to pull into the hotel driveway, though there wasn't as much traffic going their way as there was ours, but it was just as bright and there would be cars passing around them with their horns going. Have a little girl, teach her about life.

Right. It was the sort of place everyone would spend their entire lives to try to spend the night there, whether it was the same reason as ours, to get kicked out, but we couldn't get kicked out of a place that we couldn't get into in the first place. We started and stopped again outside the bar at the bottom of the hill down from the hotel with the same name, Chateau Marmont begetting Bar Marmont. Some girls were standing outside in their short skirts waiting to be shown in, but none of them looked like they should be there. I mumbled, A girl is the mother of the man. They might have seemed to belong if they were being seen to then fanned with the same palm fronds that had been transplanted to the city in the hotel's lifetime, but they wouldn't be shown in. It's all plastic.

It's a beautiful empty city filled with beautiful empty people.

The play's the thing and all the men and women only things.

Huh.

It's all plastic and plastic dicks. The light ahead turned and we were on our way until another light turned another way and we stopped. I cleared my throat and said, This city is all lines.

Speaking of girls. Did you fuck Audra.

No, I think it's one of those love-hate sorts of loves. A schizophrenic Scheherazade.

I could've fucked her already, the way she's always laughing at everything I say.

Does she even know who you are.

It was bright enough outside to tell that it was the middle of the night. The light changed as he tried to move over to make a left turn, taking a while getting there with the traffic on one side not letting him in and all the ones behind swerving around. We turned and the street unwinded into a straightaway unlike the strip before, nothing up ahead and nothing for him to do but swerve back and forth for himself.

Dun dun.

He laughed and made the sound again like there was an orchestra behind him.

Dun dun.

He shifted into the left lane some.

Dun.

He shifted back into the right lane.

Dun.

Come on man, I don't wanna die again. Where should we go.

Do you wanna go back to the Roosevelt.

Yeah, why not. No girls there.

Adam straightened out with the road and drove the rest of the way without us saying anything, the wind blowing in and out of the windows again. A little girl was all of creation. Everyone else was already leaving when we turned off of Hollywood Boulevard to find parking where we could still see the bright red neon of the Hotel Roosevelt sign in the darkness that the white lights made out of the night.

Adam walked ahead of me as I was feeling it much more than before but not as bad. It had taken longer than last time when I felt like I was dying and I could see everything for what it was then and even what it wasn't, which wasn't what I wanted, no, I had told myself I wanted to feel dumb and I wanted to feel numb, which I could and it was good.

We were in the lobby of the Hotel Roosevelt and Adam was in the middle where there was the fountain no one could sit near without getting wet. He circled around it three quarters of the way, looking at what the women looked like, but most of them were drinking in couples on the leather couches that were moved into the lobby in the night when it was turned into a bar. He came back around and I cut across to catch up to go to the counter in the corner closer to the concierge.

Should we go back for the bottle, I asked him.

No, come on.

There were more of them standing along the counter than sitting at the high stools, already far into their nights, the ones who weren't in pairs much louder than the others, looking for Adam or someone as young as him to make the most of the delusion that they weren't really as old as they said they weren't. When the bartender got to us, Adam asked for waters, which the bartender then took his time with to talk to the other drinkers. Drinking was waiting, waiting for the drink to get there and waiting for someone to drink with, waiting to get another drink and waiting for the end of the night. The bartender wasn't dressed as well as any of the bartenders last night, but the two waters he brought us with too much ice and a slice of lime looked more like a gin and tonic than anything I might have made.

Adam thanked the bartender then leaned against the counter to sip his water and when I drank from mine without the straw he told me, Don't drink too much and you won't have to buy a drink and then we'll meet some ladies to buy us whatever they're drinking.

Right, I'd hate to kill the buzz I've got going.

It gets too obvious after a while, asking for that many waters. Keep up the illusion that you're actually drinking alcohol. Try to drink slow.

It was a step to the side from his usual one and done, but Adam didn't need anything to drink, any drug to take. It would only sober him up from his natural state. Unaltered he was unlike anyone I knew. He only needed something in his hand to talk to someone.

Should we make the rounds then, I asked.

I like it here, but yeah.

I like the whole art décor sort of thing they have going on here.

Let's go to the Library Bar.

Adam went ahead again and I followed him to the other corner of the lobby where there was a small side bar that was dimly lit with a wall of mirrors that made it look large but intimate. It was loud enough for the ones with so much to say but nothing worth saying, their mouths moving and unheard by the ones who kept their faces in their own mirrors. There were bookshelves but it was too dark to read or to see if the books were real. I sipped my water while Adam tried but couldn't pass the ones waiting for their drinks at the counter and the ones in line to get to the bartenders in fedoras who picked at a pair of still lifes for the drinks they mixed, which were always set on fire then handed to someone to drink warm. Adam set his water down on a bookshelf to straighten his jacket and pull on his shirt sleeves to show through the ends.

Why's it called the Library Bar, I asked him.

I tried to stay there to not seem like I was only with Adam when he shrugged and headed back to the lobby, but there was nothing to steal and nothing I could afford to ask for, so I stayed for a second then went back to the lobby. I walked through the arranged couches and went to stick my hand in the cold fountain water before going back to the main bar again. Adam had asked another bartender for another water then asked me for someone else to hear, Do you want anything.

No I'm okay for now.

Let's go outside then.

The bartender came back with Adam's drink and Adam nodded at him. He looked to me and I waved him off. Adam held his glass up to mine and we drank, but we didn't toast to anything.

Why don't you go ahead, I told him. I'll come in a little while.

Yeah that's a good idea. He patted me on the shoulder. I'll see you in a bit.

Adam shook my hand and left as I sat down on a stool and wasn't sure what I was doing there, maybe waiting to go back to the car for something to drink before I followed him, but he had the keys on him. I stared up at the Spanish style mezzanine and reached in my pocket to take another pill, making sure to take one every one to two hours unless there was a missed dose and I would then have to take three to five every hour until I was caught up to the right dosage. I drank it down with my drink and put my hand on the counter to get off the stool and keep my balance while I floated down onto my feet, staring at the glass to make sure I didn't spill as the hotel started to spin and I turned the other way to not be taken with it, walking with the fountain in my hand, I took another drink, swallowing it slowly and trying not to drown, closing one eye then the other then both and I looked at the stars in my head, the water at my toes.

I took a step and a deep breath and didn't feel bad.

The Tropicana Bar was one floor down from the lobby then down a hallway and straight ahead past the concierge and left then straight again and if there wasn't a line it was a good night. Every thing spun back into place and I went downstairs and down the hallway and passed the concierge and nodded at them, turning left and going straight again to take another pill because there wasn't a line, going ahead to the front of it to go outside into the Tropicana, all the palm trees and the outdoor heaters left outside and all their shadows from the lighted pool of blue-green water.

I walked around it and the farther I went the more of them I could see at the counter, Adam at the end already talking to a pair of women. They looked good to me as I went over to the three of them and finished my water. There was some soft jazz music but no band to look at and I smiled at the brunette and the blonde and turned to Adam.

He told me, Why don't you go buy her a drink. He stopped me. Don't get too drunk.

I'm not drunk.

But don't get too drunk.

Fuck off.

Him and the brunette went one way as the blonde took me by the hand to the counter where it wasn't too crowded for the number of bartenders behind it. She ordered something and I said that I would have the same. She squeezed my hand and stared at me closely as she told me how old I looked for how young I was, the older one looked when one was young, the younger one looked when one was older. I smiled in the shallows until the drinks came and I didn't let go of her hand to give her her drink, finding a rolled up bill in my pocket to leave with a bartender I couldn't see well enough to tell how much I would have given her if I could. The drink was a tropical one and it was red.

We turned to go and she led me to the other side of the pool to sit where it was darker and we were alone. I drank and it was good what she ordered. I asked her her name and she said, Diane.

Diane spoke with a thick laryngitic drawl she pushed past her thin reddened lips that were so red they almost weren't. She sounded like a lounge singer from when the Hotel Roosevelt was somewhere to be and she sounded like she had started smoking when she was a little girl.

How old do you think I am. She stared at me and a little while later said, Honey. It was a little too late that it just lingered in the air where it was and I tried not to but I stared right back at her for the longest time. She looked like she could have said anything, that she might have even said she was older than she was only to hear someone say they thought she was younger than that, all the while hoping that that would be younger than what she really was, but even if she might have said she was younger than me, I would tell her I was too old for her too. I stared at her for a long enough time that it might have affected how old I said she was, but still I couldn't say.

I told her, I don't know.

Why don't I give you a window. Everything she said sounded as though she was asking something like she already knew what it was. Between fifteen and fifty. What she said came out more like, Between fifty and fifty. It then hung in the air for a while like, Fifty-fifty. Those odds weren't half-bad, no, they were as good as any and as even.

I don't know, I'm no good at this sort of thing.

It's okay. She laughed then covered her mouth to cough. It's better you say nothing at all.

I think I can do that, I said and laughed with nothing else to say and just drank instead.

She stared at me how I had at her and we could both tell that what we were doing was getting old right then. Her eyes were as blue as they always were and brighter than anything else she was wearing with her round gold earrings and her blonde-in-a-bottle hair and her silvery sequin dress that was tight on her body. She looked good sitting poolside as away

from the rest of them as we were, the only light there coming
up through the water. She had her heels off between us, but
still I sat crosslegged while she had already sunk her feet into
the pool until they seemed smaller than they were, like a little
girl's feet and like she had found the fountain of youth and
still was testing the water.

What're you doing now.

The jazz samba playing from the Tropicana Bar wasn't too
soft to not hear over the rest of them who were all the same
in the way they didn't age but were older than they really were,
wished for eternal youthfulness and were given immortality
instead, all of them blonde and blond and sober, but sure of
what they were doing and not who they were. There they were
in an older Hollywood they acted like they had always been a
part of, all the motherfuckers and all the motherfucks, all of
their sybilence Cumaean, none of them with nothing to say.

What am I doing now, I asked. I looked away from the
Cumaean women and the buzzing they made with the samba
and the rest of them who talked over it almost with the sound,
syncopatedly without hearing what they said as much as they
tried, whispering to each other how they wished they were
dead. What am I doing, I asked her as much as myself without
sounding how she did.

Diane wasn't one of the Cumaean women. Her age looked
good on her like getting old wasn't a life and death thing as
much as a way to pass the time. I stared at her feet and at the
pool and at the bottom of the pool painted with blue curved
lines a few feet long and covered in them, almost one line for
everyone there at the Tropicana Bar. They curved toward
each other and fit together to break like waves where there
shouldn't have been any if not for being frescoed there.

Yes.

I'm poolside at the Roosevelt. None of them knew of the
waves the colored and chromosomal lines looked like and
how the pool was covered with one for almost everyone

there. What would they have said if they had known about their brief lines at the bottom of that pool, one for all the good ones who died, one for all the good ones who were still alive, maybe that was that for them, all the good ones died while all the ones still alive in their old Hollywood were afraid they might just live forever. I'm talking to you.

She had been watching me, but she didn't say much when she did and I couldn't hold her stare, so I looked down at the water. I told her, I'm drinking with you. No, I'm drunk with you.

She smiled.

I'm not sure what I am doing right now really.

She stared at her feet in the water like she was seeing them for the first time. What I meant to say was. She talked over everything else and it was hard to hear anything under her. What do you do. She drank and the jazz music was there again as the rest of them tried to talk over it. What do you do for a living.

Oh, I don't know.

She smiled for me to say something better and leaned into me to hear me better or just to lean into me when she heard what I said, but maybe it was just cold where we were, the poolside itself made up of thick slabs of stone that seemed to have been found the way they were then fit together, hot enough on one's feet during the day to want to dive in, not holding onto that same heat too long into the night to keep one from diving in the pool to see if it might be warmer. The stones were dark gray and shaped like slate.

What're you on, she asked me.

I'm not on anything. This is me.

That's too bad.

Why, did you want some.

If you're gonna be adorable about it.

I tried telling her I couldn't really say what I did. She turned away to cover her mouth and she coughed and must have been cold. There were the heat lamps closer to the counter, but I couldn't feel much, but then again her heels were already off and her feet wet. I said, I'm thinking maybe I should be a struggling artist.

Oh. She smiled and I couldn't really tell what she meant to say by that then she leaned back to reach into her purse. It was getting late enough at the Tropicana for the rest of them to be all over each other. She was there in front of me again and offered me a silver cigarette wallet, but I held my hand up to say no. She smiled and took one of her cigarettes and held it to her thin lips before going back into her purse as the song ended and all of them stood around with nothing to do.

There was only their talking to each other and there was her lighting her cigarette then there it all was as loud as before.

A struggling artist, she said. She put her lips together like she was about to kiss something but then let go of the smoke and it went for a while before it turned into nothing, well before it had to reach any of the rooms, which was hard to know with the Roosevelt Hotel all around us and most of the rooms dark, but she said it like she had heard that as many times as she had heard someone say they were going to be in the pictures. She asked me, Why not just be an artist.

Back at the bar two of them had gotten loud to fight over someone and I looked but listened to her backtrack to say something about the struggling fitting me. She hadn't turned and didn't want to see what was going on, so it was good that I was alone with someone and that it was someone like her that we could talk.

I think that's true, but I'd rather say I'm struggling than do something about it now. You know, if it ends up being one thing or another, at least I only have my feet in the water for now.

Her toenails were painted red like a little girl's toes and they wiggled in the water and her feet were bright in the light from the pool.

You don't even have your shoes or socks off yet.

No, yeah, you're right.

She leaned into me and pulled on one of my shoelaces until it came undone and she laughed. I took off my shoe and my sock after to slip it inside, sitting crosslegged with the one shoe on then waited until it seemed like she wouldn't undo the other one, so I took the shoe off myself then the other sock and put the pair next to each other like someone standing up straight. She splashed her feet out of the pool and curled her toes before dropping them in again, maybe I should have done the same, but I thought of going back to the bar to get another drink when the time came, though looking at the Tropicana there wouldn't have been enough room in the pool if all of them wanted to dive in. I reached for her hand and she gave it to me. I held onto it and spun her wedding ring slowly around her finger so the small diamonds faced her palm.

Is there a Mrs. Diane, I asked.

Yes I am that Mrs. that is spoken for.

That's alright. I like to drink with people I don't know that won't remember me. All the good ones though, isn't that what they say.

My sister is getting married actually. We're here for the weekend to look at dresses.

That was your sister back there.

Yes.

Is she one of the good ones.

Of course.

She doesn't look like you.

No, but she is my sister.

That's good, Diane. Diane.

Yes.

Diane, what's Diane short for, is it short for Diandrea.

It's long for Anne.

That's a good one.

There wasn't much left of the half-cigarette still in her hand that she had gone through quicker than I expected, though cigarettes were after all supposed to take a few minutes off the end of the smoker's life, maybe because they made one move forward through time too fast for oneself and maybe they had one move backwards from the end at the same time, but even if it was the second I had seen her go through since we met, it was how she went through them like she was in a rush to meet herself halfway that it must have saved her a few minutes from smoking her cigarettes or at least had her break even in the end.

What sort of art, she asked.

I don't know. I'm not too sure what's left to do. It's all been done already like there hasn't been anything that hasn't already been redone. I had neared the end of my drink, so I finished it as she took her hand away from me and turned to cough, which sounded worse that time. If I wanted to do something good all I'd have to do is something done half a century ago. I must have sounded better to her when I hadn't said as much, but she finished her drink and set it down. I sounded as interesting as any one of them at the Tropicana and sounded like I was reading off a script, though they were at their most interesting when all their lines were scripted, not wishing they were dead but dumb and numb.

Nostalgia is still something isn't it.

It is.

But saying nothing is new is nothing new.

Isn't it.

It isn't.

She looked like Marilyn Monroe if she had lived for another handful of years. I almost said it to her but didn't because she must have almost gotten that all the time, no, Diane looked like she could have been anyone with her big brown eyes and short straightened hair. Her hair looked red in the light from the pool. She looked like the Devil in a dress.

She reached over me and rolled up one of my pant legs to my knee. She did whatever she wanted to do then I did the other one too.

The music shifted into something of a swing led by the sound of a train leaving a station and I asked her, What is that the Chattahoochee choo choo.

She looked over at the bar and said, More like the Chatta-hoochee cha cha.

Yeah I suppose all those songs have trains in them.

She smiled then a while later asked me again, So what sort of art.

I don't know. Do you know when frescoes stopped being the thing to do.

Wouldn't you rather do something set in stone rather than painted on it.

I should have been someone rather than try to do something.

But I think frescoes stopped being the thing to do much more than half a century ago, right.

Yeah, but everything we know is reversed. To be ahead of one's time is to be behind.

She smiled and told me, I hope you don't forget me. I won't forget you.

But I'm nothing. I'm nobody. No one.

That's three things you are already.

I laughed. Women are better when they're older.

Young men are better when they don't talk so much.

I'm not that young.

I'm not that old.

Right.

She stared at me while she smoked and there was nothing else to do but drink the water left in my glass and look at her too, from where we were there was nothing else to see, but then she had my wrist in her hand and pulled me to her, which I let her do with my feet crossed under me and nowhere else to go. She had her cigarette in her offhand and tried to lean me into her the way she would into me and she put her lips together and looked like she was about to kiss something, but when I stopped letting her and leaned in myself, she pulled me off balance with my eyes already closed to kiss something and when I opened them again I was in the pool without a struggle and she kissed nothing. I had held onto my drink and it was full of water and I looked up and I could see her feet, that they were the way they were, trying to see the rest of her, but the light from the pool had turned everything dark with how bright it was in there. I let go of the cup and it sank to the bottom of the pool, kicking my legs and straightening my body to come to the top and it was loud again as she sat back laughing like she hadn't meant to do it. She looked at everyone else to notice where I was with my clothes still on, but no one did and I reached up to grab at her ankles and she was really laughing then and I was too once she was in the pool with me. She sank down and came up again with her hair slicked back and still holding onto the half of a half-cigarette as she whispered into my ear how old she was and if I were to put her into a fresco to leave it out so she would live forever, so I told her I would. We sank down together as her hair came up around her and seemed like it would stay that way always, my tie coming up slowly above me, I pressed it down against my shirt and buttoned the top two buttons of my jacket to keep it where it was all supposed to be, her red lipstick ran and her smile came off her lips, letting go of her cigarette, we watched it rise slowly like smoke, but it wouldn't go much farther than the top of the pool and it wouldn't reach the red neon Roosevelt Hotel sign, though wasn't it the Hotel Roosevelt or was it the Roosevelt Hotel or did it even make a difference if the sign said one thing and they all called it something else. Maybe we would go to her cabana room at the other end of the Tropicana when we were done or maybe she didn't have a cabana and we would go home and maybe it would be together and maybe it wouldn't be and maybe we would get a cabana or maybe we would drown right where we were.

INTERLUDE
HIGHWAYMEN

The lost ones—Adam they say add em—we're the lost ones. The lost ones are all other outcomes in our heads when we've come up tails. They're nothing to see, but we hear them. They speak for me and they're the chorus—breathe they say speak—and they're the voices in your heads when I have lost my head.

I lie dead.

I come to and I can hear a faint singsong voice telling me about the end but then it stops when she coughs and clears her throat then hums before she starts again, the voice of an angel of death. Everything hurts too much to roll onto my front, but either way I'm tied down. My right eye a slit I can't see much out of how swollen it is, the right side of my body hurting from shoulder to hip, the senses in order are taste, touch, smell, sound, sight then pain and pleasure at one end and the other with time moving between all of them. My hand hurts to raise up to my mouth, but I cough into it, almost choking on my Adam's apple then swallowing it down to stick in my throat again. I taste the blood and look at my hand and see it's red—breathe they say bleed—but I don't know which one bloodied the other while I pass in and out for some time.

I can hear her singing in my head.

My suit is stuck to my skin and I've sweated into its thin fibers, too tired to shiver but too cold to fall asleep again. It must be past midnight because my tie isn't around my neck but bunched up in my shirt pocket, a breast flowering from my chest that I fondle and I'm half hard, maybe from the road rumbling under me, lying down I can feel it all over as I stretch myself to my full length, the measure of death—six feet under they say six feet over—as I look up out of the back window but see nothing, instead I close my eyes to stare at the night sky I know—Orion becomes Orionid they say the hunter becomes the hunted—and I feel cold because all the water that was inside me has been sweated out of me as if I've been unbaptized and turned inside out to dry.

I ask Adam if he hears her singing and where the girls we were with are and where are we going without them.

He doesn't hear me and I pull the chair back forward to hear him better. My life was this move from the backseat to the front and from the right to the left, but I've moved back to the right and I am the passenger again, neither the child nor the father. I sit forward and stare up ahead to see we must have shot the moon, the star-spangled night mourning at the other end of the sky like it may turn into tomorrow right in front of us, taking all the other constellations with the names I know I used to know with it, having emptied them like the last white headlights we haven't seen in some time before the sky turns blue, no, no more white headlights coming at us and no red taillights to follow, though we're still driving somewhere in the city—whir they say word—but no one else is out here anymore and we're on our way out too.

In the beginning—interlude they say introlude—in the end.

Los Angeles is a highway running to San Francisco on an old road called the Royal Road that is older and longer than anyone might know. It is the one I created coming out of the crater—crater they say cradle—in Chicxulub where all the dinosaurs died, where I covered their world in ashes and dust, where I became the last feathered serpent. It is the one I led the conquistadors on out of the Yucatán, searing their flaming swords and swearing their words—to look for gold they say to look for God—west and north to Tenochtitlan, where I led all the king's horsemen chasing the gods and bringing their death, half horse and half man, the Americans wouldn't know where our heads were, where we ended or they began, but knowledge is death and ignorance is God. It is the one I drove to Teotihuacan, the serpent setting on the sides of the pyramid step by step, the one I swam from the Sea of Cortés and to the island of California—west and north they say back and forth—where I settled onto the road snaking through the valley and over the mountains to the sea. I see I've shed my skin. I am as Ouroboros—either oroboros they say neither noroboros—as I am not. I am the serpent circling up the tree, the branches appear and disappear then reappear larger as if they were the trunk rooting the tree. I am the serpent snaking up your spine, coiling you—coil us they say call us—the branches. I am the serpent circling moments of endlessness, the lost ones.

I don't know the words, but her humming is still in my head.

Adam shakes me awake and I'm there again and he asks me if I am awake. He doesn't take his eyes off the road and he doesn't have to. We're on the 101—one oh one they say true false true—nearing the end of a stretch called the Hollywood Highway where the northwest road takes a turn for us to either go north or west. We can be certain which way we're going, if not ever where, but in such a moment of uncertainty we're everything we are and will be. We're in the middle of it all going northwest before we either take a turn to go north and straight through the state or take the other turn and go west to wind along the ocean, but for now we are both where we are and where we aren't.

She isn't here, but I can hear her.

The 101 runs north and south and east and west and every direction in between. We would go west in search of golden gods and see the sea and sea monsters. We would go north to the bridge and see what is red when they say it is golden. We would go south down to the river and seek out the tree of life or east across America to the fountain of youth.

I say to him to go east young men.

He tells me to go west you mean.

Adam was right. These are all the sorts of immortality that would only last one a lifetime. It is best not to go west and north and back and forth—south and east they say see the beast—but east and south to the mouth makes as much sense because the tree of life and the tree of knowledge of good and evil are but branches.

Where were we and when will we get there. The road stretches out in front of us about as far as I can see that we aren't where we should be, no, the road is laid bare and is nothing to see yawning against another dusky dawn waiting at the end of itself. It isn't the 101 we're on now but the 5.

It outstretches us with so much behind us that I can tell we must have already made it through the mountains then down into the straight and narrow highway that is bound north and south and not much else through the Central Valley. We are bound with it now in the way of man. We are as far and away from the coastal curves of the 101 as we could ever be, not snaking along the ocean but unwinding ourselves inland where we can see how the line grows longer but always stays the same shape, as fast as it is on the 5, fast only in the way men measure time, the way of mortality, the way of highwaymen trying to steal as much of it as they can at night when the stuttered white lines on the road have a visible end in one's own light.

The night had left us here somewhere between sunset and sunrise staring at what was once the sliver of light circling the horizon until it died—from the farther they say and from the son—then the sun rising made the white lines on the road grow brighter and brighter until they reached into the nothing at the end of the road. We drive though. We drive though man may never make a line as straight as the serpent, though juxtaposition is the only sort of composition man made, though similarity is the same difference, though the creation of man is only ever turning everything into everything else.

Everything is everything and nothing. The truth is that good and bad are good, which is to say, truth isn't always what it sounds like, though good is still good and bad is still bad, but man made of nature as he is, the nature of man is to undo his nature, turn his symmetry into asymmetry, but symmetry and asymmetry both make a symmetry. There are two branches like two horns coming out of our heads—one is the past they say one the future—and all we ever do is butt horns. There are two selves, one the creator of life and all possibility of goodness, one the destroyer of words and the probability of badness, one the poetic and one prosaic, one life and one death. They are I. Let us be mouthbreathers of I.

I is God and me.

I is Adam and Eve.

Let us purge ourself and begin again then. The reader is the writer and writing is rewriting and repetition is repetition. One would breathe the voices in our heads, for we are much too much for ourself, for we aren't much more than mulch— mulch too much they say mulch to mulch—for we are branches branching and the tree itself self-symmetry. The spine bending back to go round and round and where we end we begin and where we begin we do not end, though we know all things must come to an end that they may begin again— ashes to ashes they say dusk to dust—when the middle is the beginning and the end, the way in is the way out and the internal the eternal and we are nothing if not everything.

I smell the ocean. To truly see the sea one has to not see the shore for a while, whether it is the ocean of man or the ocean before him. It isn't here for me to see, but here all the same—hear they say say—since there is no order to the senses when to speak is to sound—oral they say aural—and to speak is to turn one sense into three orifices—to mouth is to hear they say the mouth is the ear—and the mind is the mouth of madness. All the senses come together in the synesthetic life. All of the tenses come together as much. The synesthetic life turns the present into the past and the past to the present. I think therefore I thought and I am because I was.

Adam says it smells like shit. I say to breathe through your mouth so you won't smell the shit. He rolls down the window then up and down again, but it does nothing. The ocean has all turned to shit. It smells like shit. I breathe through my mouth slowly to try not to breathe out my insides while Adam says it's all the livestock we're passing on the side of the road. I look at the cattle but I'm drifting in and out. I tell him I think I'm suffering from synesthalgia. I'm having one of those surrealizations they always said I would. How much more measured my manias have become for me to recognize them. The stream of consciousness deltas the sea of unconsciousness.

The white line repeats itself against the road. The 101 and the 5 are one in the same as there is no truth to the senses, so to speak to someone else is to turn one sense into five orifices. Speak of the Devil and my ears burn into horns—the reader is the writer they say the either is the either—but I am the Devil and I am not. That we might—heads or tails they say tails never fails—or that we might not is a fear always at our heels, but certainty is the fear of nonexistence spread by the boolean soothsayers and their true-or-false prophets of the binary pantheon. The beauty of uncertainty is lost in the vanities of certainty. We are not predetermined nor predestined but rather predisposed. We are at odds with ourself to see things as they are, no, not as one but as ones, if we are to know that oneself is but one of all ones as all the others are the lost ones. We are true and false and truth. We shall not surely die.

I am the fall of man.

I am the leviathan—the beast of the belly they say the belli of the beast—as I am the serpent.

I am plumed.

I am Apophis.

We are one in the same if the odds of the asteroid Apophis ending the world, one in the sort of numbers that don't matter, do matter, if not the ones in line beneath the one, if not the repetition of the odds, if not the lost ones.

I come to and I'm half hard again, but we're sitting still and something smells good. I smell it, the smell of driving to somewhere, it takes me back. Gasoline is the smell of death—breathe through your mouth they say not through your nose—but it is now stuck in my head, the brain cells dying and someone saying to me when I was a child that gasoline is laced with the smell of death.

The windows are rolled down and it is cold. My suit itches and I strain to sit up to reach for the handle and get out of the car to stretch, losing my balance and landing against the door, my entire body hurts this time, but I stand up straight and look around to see no one is there to see the spectacle of me bending my knees up and down and stepping in circles to learn how to walk again. A few times around the car and I walk away from the station, down and up a dirt ditch, closer to the highway where I can look at both ends and wonder which way we're headed. There are groves of some sort of citrus trees in both directions and several other stations on the other side of the road. All the stations are covered for worse weather than now and brightly lit for how early it is in the morning, but they'll have to turn off the lights soon. I head back to the car where it's parked next to pump number sixteen of sixteen and I can't tell if the smell is getting to me, but it feels good to think we're going somewhere while I keep smelling the gasoline since either way I was born with too many brain cells that it would be a waste for me not to kill a handful.

Several trailers pass by and I watch them for a while then Adam comes out of the station and I go to the pump and reach for the nozzle, coming back around to put it in the tank, pull the trigger back and listen as the gasoline rushes downstream into the car and I breathe through my mouth—so they don't feel dumb they say so they don't feel numb—and exhale the nothing. Adam tells me he took some money for gas out of my jacket. I feel my breast pocket then I pull my tie by its tail out and ball it up again and put it in my pants pocket and I tell Adam that I didn't know I had any cashish. He shrugs and says nothing. Adam is different when one of us isn't drunk. As high as his highs are his lows are lower.

I walk back and forth then feel disjointed and I sit down again and roll up my window. I don't remember how to fall asleep, if it works to count backwards from one hundred and one, one hundred and nothing, no, I'm too tired to keep counting. I struggle to breathe again. One of the older ones once tried to strangle me in the churchyard and I started to hit him until there was nothing I saw but white and when they brought me in I told them I don't remember what I did, so they told me about heaven and they told me about hell again, but I was afraid of both, both such absolutes, I always tried to play to both sides, God and the Devil, to be good enough to be left alone by one and to be bad enough to be left alone by the other, but a child can only play the odds for so long. I try not to remember childhood too much because it's all untrue one way or another—tra la la la they say trauma mama—but we repeat ourselves in our memories to have a narrative that makes sense to someone other than ourself, repeat our memories in our heads until they ring truer to us too, turning truth into untruth into another truth. We are things of nothing.

The nozzle clicks and I get up to unhook the car. Adam says he has to go piss and I tell him to get the change too and he asks me if I want anything to eat and I tell him not really no but if they have beer to get some. Adam tells me he was afraid he'd have had to give me a Vicodin funeral—viking they say Odin—but I say I wouldn't have minded being set out to sea, so he walks back to the station and I take out the tie from my pocket, pulling the nozzle from the car and letting loose some of the leftover gasoline into the tie before I put the nozzle back into the pump. I sit down to smell the tie. The American Dream is a coma. Let us be mouthbreathers and let us be dumb.

The end will come when nothing is neither too good nor too bad, but one should be good if one is good and one should be bad if one is bad and one should be true to an end. Life is valued more than a good life. They have made a drug of life and turned us into addicts. They tell us that life is immortality, no, I say immorality is immortality. They make nothing but nothing of nothing. The sort of immortality that doesn't come from a tree. Mother branches make daughter branches and daughters make mothers. I hear her faint singsong voice again.

Adam gets back and I close the door and the engine turns over several times then the smell of going somewhere is gone when we get on the road again, but the high is on its way. I hold the tie in my hand and cover my face. Andrea smelled like gasoline. Adam tells me that we're more than halfway there and I tell him less than halfway. I breathe the tie in and out again. Andrea again. In the word of God, to know is to fuck. God is a four letter word—oh they say God—for the lack of a better word. I knew Andrea but didn't know her well. I roll the window down and the air rushes into my lungs so I don't have to think about breathing or not—we want to feel dumb they say we want to feel numb—and for the time being I let the synesthetic turn into the anesthetic. We're the lost ones because we're still alive—Andrea they say Andreas— while she is everything she was and I am anything and I am nothing. The ands justify the ends. *An*drea or An*dr*ea—tree they say tre—an or on, no, and.

Andrea.
Andread.
Anddead.
Anddread.
Andrend.
Andred.

THE LOST ONES
PART TWO

We're here, Adam said shaking me awake. He had his hand on my shoulder to shake me back and forth with my neck stretching from side to side and feeling good until my head hurt up and down then started hurting everything else. Wake the fuck up, motherfuck.

I fell out of the door but didn't hit the street because of the seatbelt holding me back. Adam laughed and went around to the back and I heard the trunk open. It was too bright to tell what time it was, but it must have taken us longer than it should have to get here. I undid the buckle and fell to the ground as the belt rewound slowly across my stomach and back inside the car while I rubbed my eyes awake. The morning was cold but not as cold as it could have been.

Am I still alive, I asked. Everything hurts. I suppose that means I'm alive.

Adam said something about us wearing our suits.

Where are we, I asked. I looked up and down the street and I said, I used to live somewhere around here.

Adam said something about Berkeley.

I stood most of my weight up against the car and my suit still felt wet. I emptied my pockets and everything on me was ruined, so I left it all in the sun on the roof. I tried to get out of my suit as Adam laughed at me struggling to undress and I knew I couldn't take my suit off if I tried. He was already jacketless and unbuttoning his shirt to rub his belly with a childish smile. I would have cursed him if I could have thought of something to say, but I couldn't and I buttoned up my jacket again and filled my pockets with my things and I stood up straight and had to piss bad.

There was a beer bottle left in the sleeve of the swung open door, so I started to finish it and it was warm. I closed the door and drank some of the beer and it was bitter as I went around the car to a house with hedges and a tree out front to piss against the trunk and the roots. I looked to see there was no there to see me.

Adam had started across the street and up the sidewalk to the wrong one and I yelled after him that it was the blue one with the windows. He saluted the air and went back and up the few steps to the blue house with the white trimming and all the windows, the second house over from the street corner with a stop sign and never much traffic. The ends of Adam's untucked shirt waved behind him as he went to the door, but he didn't know anyone there and I didn't know if anyone was even home.

I looked back and forth and listened to the stream hissing against the tree while drinking from the bottle and I felt like one of those fountains with the cherubs always pissing themselves just to refill the fountain and piss themselves again. It was taking a long time to finish and maybe it was me drinking the beer that kept it going, but I didn't stop. There was the time we were in between bars and I turned on some side street and let the car neutral for Adam to steer while I went to piss on a tree then came running after the car, which had idled halfway down the street, but that was a long time ago—Adam they say annum—and since then Adam had told me he had started to drink his own urine, which was best to do in the morning when there was the most melatonin and what one had to do is piss to let the start of the stream kill the bacteria on the head before filling a cup to drink, but I couldn't remember all the things Adam had told me that I didn't want to remember. I shook from the piss shivers or from the cold and looked at the trunk and roots and the grass and some of the concrete that had been covered in my urine and I left the bottle in the gutter and went back to the car and took my bag out and put it on the street then I looked at the house and put the bag back in and took an unopened beer bottle out and closed the trunk.

Adam was outside again and shirtless down the steps to stand by a tree at the street side of the sidewalk opposite the dark purple and white flowers in the small garden at the front of the house where another leafless tree branched over the side of the stairway with some bicycles left slanted and locked to the rails leading up to the house. I went across the street and saw Adam didn't look as tired for as long as he had been driving, but then again there was no need to get there too early and if he had turned off on the side of some road to sleep it must have done him some good.

Are you gonna bring your things in, he asked me.

I don't think so.

I think I might.

Okay.

Are we gonna stay here.

I think so, but we don't have to.

It's not bad here, it's good. It's what we want for now.

Sounds good.

He went to get his things as I went to the stairs to hold the head of the bottle against the curled end of the handrail, fitting it against the edge, hitting it a few times with my fist until the cap shot off foaming and I drank until it stopped.

The stairs were covered in the morning sun and chipped blue paint several shades lighter than the house itself. The last time I had been inside was a year and not too long ago on something of a bender that had gotten bent before I went back home. It had been long enough for everyone there to forget everything I couldn't remember to begin with, but I walked slowly up to the porch where I saw leaning in the doorway Saint Francis in his boxer briefs, as bright a red as how well they fit him, his stomach just covering the top of the elastic that held them there, though it might have been his stomach itself that kept his underwear on him. He looked like a newborn.

Saint Francis.

My son, he said crossing me then coming in for a hug to lift me and spin me around once and I thought I would throw up as I handed him the bottle. He drank and said, Bless you.

Saint Francis of San Francisco, lead us into temptation.

You're early.

I didn't know you were expecting us.

Neither did I.

I laughed.

You look about as bad as one can in a suit, he said and he laughed too.

Saint Francis was Saint Francis because he was some years older than everyone else but wiser too because he was where we were in life and had been there some years longer and he was wise enough to stay there as long as he had. He was Saint Francis since his name shortened to Francis and because he lived down the street from the rest of them, which made him a few blocks closer to San Francisco, making him Saint Francis of San Francisco or Saint Francis for short. Nobody called him Saint Francis but me.

Happy New Year to you too.

Was that yesterday already.

Yesteryear, I think.

Is that right.

I don't know. What time is it.

Almost noon.

Really, I asked looking up for the sun.

Like almost an hour until noon.

That sounds about right.

He smiled with his thin lips that would stretch wide with some of the stubble around them, his skin brown, his hair black but almost shaved, his eyes brown behind enameled browline glasses that always drew attention from everything else when he sometimes wore them. He looked at me like he had been out most of the night into the morning, like it didn't matter to him that we were there but that he was there. It was too early to almost be noon.

Adam was still across the street moving things in the trunk. There was a weathered couch that took up most of the porch with its back to the window, which would have looked into the kitchen if the window wasn't as dirtied as the couch was stained, gray and darker gray with a few sorts of spills. I sat down on it while Saint Francis stayed standing and took up some of the doorway with both mass and muscle from years of drinking and years of lifting things when he was drunk.

How're you holding up.

He drank from the beer and he was waking up but still not altogether there, but the beer would get him there. He lapped his tongue against the roof of his mouth then he licked his lips to say, A little hair of the dog never hurt anybody.

You're not Saint Christopher though.

I'm not anybody right now.

Hair of the dog, head of the dog.

He looked at the label on the bottle. The hair of the dog was killing his hangover and bringing him back to life, the hair of the dog the only chaser a drinker ever needs—chase the tail they say catch the head—like the hair on the dog's tail is the only thing the dog ever needs.

Come on, I said. Let me get my paws on you.

Saint Francis sat next to me and I patted him on the shoulder and he handed me back the beer.

Remember when we brought this thing back, I asked him and I drank.

The couch.

The porch couch yeah, the pouch, does everyone still call it the pouch.

He laughed and said, No one ever called it that.

It's better than the corch. I finished the beer and held it up, A little pooch on the pouch.

I remember we left it on its side to make a political statement, but in the morning you were on it passed out with some hoochiemama.

Hah I don't remember that. I just remember carrying it

from down the street.

Yeah. The things people throw away.

I peeled the label off and slid it into the bottle then sank the bottle into the divide between the couch cushions. Ignorance isn't bliss, I said. Bliss is ignorance.

Adam didn't look hungover with a suitcase in one hand and backpack on his back and a pillow under his arm as he went inside and Saint Francis followed him, waving his arms around to show Adam something or other. I wondered if I was hungover as I followed them inside and I saw how the front room hadn't changed much. The walls were still light blue but more of a canvas for their art brutesque drawings of people they knew, for their painted self-portraits with some scribblings to the side of them like the works were in a museum, for their street signs they stole. There might have been a few more of them put up over the year. Written on the wall was that found art is best stolen. One of them once said that. It might have been me. There were still the same couches that formed a capital L in the front corner. Adam had put all his things on the longer couch against the sidewall, so I strained out of my jacket and left it on the one that was shorter but more cushioned, pushed to the bay window of a front wall not looking out on the bay. There were no curtains and the sun shined on everything and in the air all the dust.

Do you have any fruit, Adam asked.

I don't know, Saint Francis said and showed him into the kitchen that opened to the left of the front room. There's something somewhere around here.

I was talking to this woman last night that works for this modeling agency and she was telling me to get in touch with her, but she was saying something about this raw diet she's on now where she essentially just eats fruit. I was telling her I was gonna go on it for a while, at first because of her being an agent that can get me a job, then because of her being a woman that could give me a job, but now I've just been feeling so fucking sick these days that I really do want to do it.

I don't know. A sudden shift like that to your system'll kill a man.

She said it'd be good for me. Is someone gonna make banana bread or something.

I think those have just been left out.

The refrigerator door opened and Adam said, I don't know.

I listened to them digging around in the refrigerator while I sat down to take off my shoes and I left them looking not bad as the only dress shoes next to the mess of the other shoes pushed into a pile behind the door that was always left open.

I knew someone who did this diet, Saint Francis said.

You bring him up like he's dead.

No, he just doesn't drink anymore, so we don't see each other anymore.

I think I'll quit drinking too.

Who quit drinking, I asked.

Me just now.

Huh, I said and laid down on my right side and it hurt and I sat up then laid on my other side.

I don't think sobriety suits you.

Not drinking is a kind of drinking, I said.

I feel like the paragon of health, nada.

Nada, Saint Francis asked.

Yeah, nada, as in, nada.

Nada, I repeated. Nada, nada, y pues nada.

Nada, Saint Francis repeated and he sounded like he was in the refrigerator. You should eat some raw fish or something too.

How long has that been there.

I don't know, as long as the bananas maybe.

Yeah these are ripe.

The fish smells ripe too.

Is there any beer in there, I sat up and asked.

It doesn't look like it.

I don't care if it's ripe or not, I said. They must not have heard me. I stood up and rolled up my sleeves and saw several raised red streaks along my forearms and I rolled my sleeves up as far as I could and saw the start of a rash I must have been scratching for some time. I unbuttoned my shirt a bit and saw the same on my chest, raised red pinpoints like bed bug bites with streaks of red over some of the patches. I buttoned up my shirt and rolled down my sleeves.

There were dozens of beer bottles and even more red and silvery-off-white and blue beer cans scattered everywhere, some of the cans in one state or another of being crushed or shortened and others looking like they belonged where they were. I went around finishing the mouthfuls of beer from the bottles and cans where they were left on the upright piano next to the longer couch and next to it the bottles and cans on a dismantled drum set, the bottles and cans on the workbench in the middle of the room, which looked like it had been cleared off for the most part before but still had a few sewing machines and other sorts of machinery at one end.

Adam came back into the front room peeling an off-black banana. He and Saint Francis sat at the workbench and Adam went on in between mouthfuls, It might've been the drive this morning that put it in my head. I'm driving and there's all these fruit trees for some time then nothing and then all of the fruit trees again, then nothing again. Dust bowl then fruit bowl. It had to be something subliminal. Fruit, nothing, fruit. Nothing but fruit repeating into the horizon.

I had stopped listening by the time I was going around to the bottles and cans left in the places where all of the dust had settled the way it did when one was too hard at work to worry about the way everything looked. Some of them felt like they were left to come back to, but I couldn't tell if they were all from last night. The sun shined through all the bottles and on all the cans and the room felt long and thin from the start of the hallway at the end.

So what now, I asked. I had had more than a few beers worth of beer before I reached the end of the room and there was one left at the top of a wood frame of an antique mirror that had been shattered and glued back together then painted with a purple and blue swirl between the leftover shards, though maybe the swirl was painted before the shards were glued back on it. The can was close to full and I sat down at the workbench with it and Saint Francis and Adam.

What now, Adam said. Nothing now. Nothing but fruit.

What're you guys gonna do, Saint Francis asked and he had some of my beer.

I don't know. We just kinda drove up for no real reason.

What happened to the oxycodone, I asked.

You happened to them.

I shrugged and held the beer can up to my mouth to drink, but the head of the can smelled like it had been inside of someone, though it might have been my fingers, which I then smelled too, but I couldn't remember anything other than drinking, so I drank.

There was OxyContin, Saint Francis asked.

There was, Adam said. He ate all of them.

How long do you think the two of you'll be here.

Maybe a week.

That sounds good.

We're thinking we might head across the country.

That sounds better.

Is there any other sort of alcohol around here, I asked and went into the kitchen that was small and mostly dirty dishes and a three-tiered spice rack with some good spices.

There's some whiskey somewhere around here. Saint Francis stood up and looked around then started for the hallway and Adam got up and followed him door to door. Saint Francis was saying something about a meaningful trip he had a month ago that made him decide to quit smoking. He had told me once the hardest part was when he was between smoking one and two cigarettes in a row when he smoked, the stage where he had one and a half cigarettes and there would be halves left around that he forgot about, but by the time he had found them again he would smoke four of the halves, lighting them one after the other, end to end. It was like fireworks.

I rinsed three glasses but couldn't find a filled ice cube tray in the freezer, so I went back to the workbench and I sat down with the empty cups. Saint Francis came back into the front room with his uneven grin and a bottle of whiskey that looked good. He poured into the three glasses.

I couldn't find any ice.

That's okay, we're mostly made up of water. No reason to go around watering down our drinks anymore than we already are.

Right, I smiled.

Adam came in and looked at the third glass and he said, I'm good.

Oh, you were serious.

Yeah, nada.

I quit drinking once, Saint Francis said. It was awful. I don't know what I was thinking, giving up drinking. I must have been drunk at the time. Saint Francis emptied the third glass into his and poured me some more too while Adam went to the couch to lie down. One for you, one for me.

Yeah. I laughed and I held my glass up to his and we drank. The bourbon burned. It wasn't as good as it looked. Smooth like avant-garde jazz.

He frowned and nodded then asked me, What do you wanna do then.

I don't know. I held my glass up again and we drank.

That'll put some bones in your body.

And take some out too.

We drank until Adam said something to himself and he stood up to go through the refrigerator again and came back from the kitchen with the rest of the bananas and ate all of them. We drank until Saint Francis decided to get dressed to start his day but then decided he might drink the day away since he had started the day that way. We drank and I had one for the road and another one for the road.

Do you wanna go somewhere, I asked.

Sure.

Where to.

We were walking around mostly keeping to ourselves in the half hour since we left without much to do in the morning. The air was good coming off the bay and inland then in and out our lungs while we wandered on and off the side streets not feeling like we were going in circles. Adam was ahead of me some and Saint Francis a way behind. We said nothing to each other and sometimes someone in front would stop and someone else would lead and sometimes someone else would fall behind.

I turned back to wait for Saint Francis to ask him if he knew if anything was open so we could get a drink, but then I saw his mouth was full with something and when he smiled there were bits of red stuck between his teeth and his mouth looked bloodied as he spat some out before running his strawberry tongue over them and yellowing his teeth again.

They're good for you, Saint Francis said and he held out his fist then opened it to a handful of flower petals. They looked like roses if not for some others mixed in and adding white to the redness. Smell good, look good. He smiled again. Taste good.

I think I'm okay for now.

He shrugged and had some more of the handful, More for me.

Adam had stopped up ahead and waited for us and when we caught up he asked, What is that.

Are you hungry.

I could eat.

Saint Francis held out the rest of his handful for Adam to try a few petals then he held out the handful to me again, so I took the rest and we kept walking. They smelled sweet and looked fine and I emptied my hand into my mouth and it was sweet to chew them and I looked back at Adam as he frowned, though it wasn't that bad, but the more I chewed the more it grew bitter and I spat it all out.

Saint Francis laughed, Yeah these aren't the best.

They're not bad at first, Adam said.

Sometimes you gotta stop to eat the roses, I said.

I didn't think you could eat flowers.

I guess it's as good a time as any for us to talk about the hummingbirds and the honeybees.

We went along and I fell behind spitting out the taste in my mouth as I salivated more and my spit had turned green. Saint Francis and Adam looked for more flowers to try some different ones that might taste as good as they looked on the bushes on the sides of the street in the wet morning air. I stopped looking down at the cracks on the gray ground or staring up at the black wires up in the sky and the soft white lines there too and I also looked for flowers. We walked and tore petals off of their buds and forced them into our mouths, the prettier they were the faster we were to try them, swallowing the good ones and spitting out the bad ones.

It's not unlike eating potpourri, Saint Francis said to me.

I've never had potpourri.

You've never had flowers either, Adam said.

Well now I've sort of had both.

Adam shrugged.

I wonder if they're some sort of an aphrodisiac.

They're the most potent one I know, Saint Francis said.

The two of them walked ahead of me as I stopped to go through a few yellow-petaled flowers I plucked from their brown-furred centers that I threw away before eating the petals, which were lacking the same bitter turn of some other flowers only because they weren't sweet to begin with—anaphrodisiac they say anaphoradisiac—so I moved on and picked through what Saint Francis and Adam had left behind, spitting to see my spit turn different colors from the flowers I just had, blue for green, yellow for white, anything but red for red. After a few more my tongue laid in my mouth swollen and itching to move, so I caught up to the two of them. Adam held onto a handful of white-tipped and blue-bottomed petals he then smelled and chewed and spat out in one motion and a frown. Saint Francis looked and talked like he was still drunk from the night before, which was the way he always looked and talked and was the morning after. Adam looked like he might have been listening, but Saint Francis talked like he was talking to no one.

I listened but walked behind them for a while and I didn't bother with any flowers because my tongue felt numbed. We crossed the next side street and I looked over to the main street one street over and I asked them, Thould we get thomething to drink.

Since when do you lithp, Adam asked.

Alwayth. I am Ulythpeeth.

What're you trying to say.

Ulythpeeth.

Ulythpeeth, Saint Francis repeated. Ulyspes.

Yeth, I think I'm thuffering from thome thort of petalergic reacthion.

Saint Francis was smelling a flower he had torn off with a few inches of stem leading up to its fleshy pink and white blossom that he spun back and forth between his thumb and forefinger and didn't put in his mouth but showed to me then stuck behind his ear as he said, I'm gonna give this to this one hoochiemama.

Girlth like flowerth.

They don't eat them though do they, Adam said.

No, not all the time.

If your breath is flowery though.

Like attracts like.

Tho try to be likeable, I said and I stuck my tongue out like a dog and panted for a while then I scraped my fingernails over my tongue several times and spat onto the concrete all the red. The puthyeaterth are alwayth philothopherth.

Saint Francis laughed and said, A rose is a rose Ciceros Ciceros.

Adam had set himself to devouring another rose bush before we turned to go up another street that felt the same as the one before, the houses the same, the cars waiting to go somewhere, most of the trees bare, the street quiet with nobody else there. We walked for a while and said nothing. Adam sometime later found several greenish-red bulbs like berries that he threw into a yard after trying one. He was the most taken with what Saint Francis had shown us right under our noses.

Poets get all the pussy, Saint Francis said to me. Are you still writing poetry.

Are you ever getting pussy, Adam asked.

Well, I'm no poet.

Why not.

You heard the nada, he doesn't get pussy.

Yeah, I drink too much. Drinking turns men into labians.

All the best poets are lesbians.

We walked for a while and thought about poetry and lesbians.

Yeah, I don't know. I sort of lost it for a while, started seeing everything as *a b a*. I still think it is, the structure you see everything in, but then everyone likes to believe that everything isn't just metered and measured out, like it isn't rhyme and repeat, rinse and repeat.

Everyone thinks they're the only one to know something about something.

Something about everything.

Everything is still something.

Maybe.

But *a b a*. Where's the other *b* in *a b a b*. It makes more sense to me to be like *a b a b*.

Then it'd just be *a b*. It's not the same.

We walked for a while and said nothing and it was a nice morning to do nothing and not have to think about it, though I kept forgetting that it wasn't morning.

Though *a b a* makes you see it as *a a b*, because *b* makes *a a*, *a* be *a*, like *b* as in be, or to be *a* okay, but that doesn't matter. None of this bullshit matters to poets. Poetry is prose like a rose.

Prosody I believe it's called, Adam said.

The best prose isn't prosaic though. It's poetic. Better isn't always best. Poets get all the pussy, though all the poets I know have pussies.

Poetesses you mean.

Poetesses get all the pussyeses.

Poetry is for the pussies, since poetry is mouthfucking. It's just the reader tonguing the poet's, poetesses' words. It comes from the feminine and they've doubled down on the feminine. All the great poets are lesbians.

Like attracts like.

I never was much of a poet, which must be why I'm not much of a pussyeater. I talk too much to make any sense. I was with this one girl and I drank too much to get hard.

You drank too much, Saint Francis asked. No, I don't believe it. We better get you into AA.

We better get you into *a b a*, Adam said.

Well, I drank more than usual then, but so I ended up going down on her, but talking too much and she must have gotten sick of hearing about all the things I wouldn't end up doing to her. That girl Audra, I said to Adam.

So you never did fuck her.

Drinking turns a man into a labian, but a bad one. Alcoholism is an androgynization.

Well you know they say you're supposed to recite the alphabet, Adam said. All the differences in mouthing all the letters, the embouchure.

The em*douche*ure.

Same difference.

But when I'm drunk, I'll be slurring all the letters. They'll come out different.

You're gonna have to learn your *a b c*'s of cunnilingus, backwards and forwards, in case you'll have to pass a breathalyzer.

I thought I told you all I see is *a b a*. That's hardly being cunnilingual.

This time come and play with me, Saint Francis said and shrugged. At least drinking'll always be there for you when you've drank too much. Saint Francis then stroked his chin and felt for the flower behind his ear. What I've learned though.

In your old age.

In my old age, what I've learned is if you want to get anywhere with a woman you should lick her feet the first time you're with her. Stick your tongue everywhere between her toes.

Like a walk on the beach, I said.

It shows you're a sexual being.

The toes are the windows to the hole.

What if she's a ballerina with ballerina toes, Adam asked.

Why bother with a ballerina, they're all virgins with no bodies.

They don't all not have bodies.

I've heard opera singers give the best head, I said. The vibrato deep down in their throats.

Yes everybody loves good oratorio, Saint Francis said.

Oratio.

You mean aria, Adam said.

If that's what you're into, you lick her feet first, she'll let you stick it in her aria.

I was gonna write an opera once, Adam said.

Yeah.

If you want to fuck you should be fucking. Women can smell if you're having sex, so if you're already having sex you can have sex. Women beget women. Fucking is everything. Saint Francis laughed higher pitched than his usual baritone and said, It's all bullshit though.

It's everything though. Motherfucking. It's always the same, two people making one person. It isn't a poem, a poem is nothing. It's done and it's there and it's nothing, though it's never done. It's this creation from oneself, it's wrestling with what might be. A sort of creation in wrestling with a lion and a goat and a serpent all at once, and instead of becoming all of them, it's a creation, not a collaboration, and life's a collaboration, but it's only this chimera, right. And what it might be. Might. A chimera.

Saint Francis laughed again, Might makes right.

It's mouthfucking, not motherfucking. No one likes a chimera, they like all the lions and goats and serpents separate. No one wants the uncertain truth, they want an agreed upon truth. All they want is all the lies. Live the lie, love the lie.

Live to love, Adam said.

Love to hate.

Hate to love, Saint Francis said and we all laughed.

So lesbians then, Adam said. Then what about gay men.

It's all either bullish or bearish.

Most of the great artists are gay, I said.

Most men are gay to some degree, Saint Francis said.

Most men aren't great to any degree.

Most gay men and at least half of all bisexuals are gay.

You know on average gay men have larger dicks than straight men, Adam said.

That makes sense, gay men are more into dicks than straight men. It's all natural selection.

I looked down at my hands and said, I don't know. A larger dick, I think I'd rather have larger hands than a larger cock. More people shake your hand than suck your dick.

Not me, Adam said. I'm terrified of germs.

I held my hand up to my face and said, I suppose a lot of it's lost in foreshortening anyway. Or I guess threeshortening.

Yeah I'm still uncircumscribed, Saint Francis said.

Still, I asked.

You never know.

Mine is more of a fiveskin, Adam said. He then walked ahead of us with a red flower that had collected some dew, which he drank from the bulb with the flower tilted back to his tongue as he made a sound to suck the few drops into his mouth. Agua dulce, he said with a childish smile.

The water of life, I said.

The sweet water, Saint Francis agreed and he approached a tree with low-hanging white petals that he tore one from and bit the head off then licked his lips.

I asked him, We're doing the lord's work aren't we muchacho.

The lord's work, yes.

What's the lord's work, Adam asked.

Creation.

Amen.

Amen.

Amen amen amen.

We walked for a while with our heads bowed down. The side street wasn't like the ones before, so we had to turn around, but we still went the circumference of the open-mouthed circle.

I said, The American Dream isn't much more than tricking you into thinking that a cul-de-sac isn't a dead end.

Cul-de-sac is a French word, Saint Francis said.

The statue de liberté was made in France, Adam said.

We need to get our hands on some narcotics.

Sure.

Smell the roses, take the doses.

I was thinking we should find some amanitas, Adam said.

Huh.

Amanita muscaria. I wanna go on one of the trips where I realize I should quit cigarettes.

But you don't smoke.

Maybe he'll take it up, Saint Francis said. I have half a carton if you wanna stop by my place.

That'd be a wrong turn for his diet.

It'd be good for us to see ourselves at this point in the journey, Adam said.

I don't like what I see when I see myself.

I've already seen myself, Saint Francis said. But I can take another look.

Yeah, maybe shave or something. I thought we were trying to lose ourselves.

We're trying to find ourselves. We should take the car to go look for some.

My car.

Your car, Saint Francis asked.

Our car.

Fuck, what we should be looking for is the tree of life.

This is the tree of life, man. Adam spun around several times with his arms extended.

We're trying to graft ourselves onto the tree of life, I said to Saint Francis. We're seeds in need of sapling.

Do you know where it's planted, Saint Francis asked.

The amanitas, Adam asked.

No, I know where those are. We have to go up in the hills. Lots of coniferous trees there.

Coniferous huh.

Yeah, the green ones.

When I was still here I used to walk around the campus looking at trees with a former plotus.

Plotus, Adam asked.

Poet laureate of the United States.

Right.

He knew all the names of all the trees and flowers and things when we walked and he told me poets know the names of things.

Should we go look for some amanitas then, Adam asked.

Let's pick up something to drink first though.

Sure, Saint Francis said.

Let's go when we get back.

Yeah let's head back.

Saint Francis walked ahead and when we got to the side street we didn't turn direction or walk any faster, though we walked with some purpose now and didn't stop to pick flowers. We walked and I fell in line with Saint Francis and felt good not to be killing time anymore.

Maybe I might get back into all the poetry again, I said. Roses are rosy, violets are violet, you are you, and I am too. Or better yet. Roses are red, violets are red, red is red, and I am red. Poetry isn't much more than prose like a rose is a rose.

It is what it is.

Adam fell behind while we crossed another intersection that formed a roundabout between the two side streets it brought together where there was a green center circle, attracting him, though it looked like grass and flowerless shrubs and weeds. Saint Francis and I didn't wait for him.

Poetry is dead, he said.

I think it's come full circle and now it is what it was, sound and words put together, sound and sense so now it's all just song. Songs are what poetry was.

Maybe I should've been a poet.

Aren't you a poet. I should've been a musician like you.

You can't make sound for sound's sake and not make sense, or make sense but sound like shit.

I just need to get the voices in my head inside other heads.

Saint Francis said nothing and we walked for a while and I looked back at Adam more than a block behind us, but we didn't bother to wait for him.

Good motherfucking mouthfucking then.

Yeah.

Motherfuck.

Motherfuck, he laughed.

Yeah, motherfuck. As in, to motherfuck. I believe it's also the name of a flower.

Oh yeah.

Well, not the Latin name. I think it's French.

We walked for a while and said nothing as the sun went behind a cloud then came out again.

There was this girl I used to know that would run her teeth up and down my cock because she never seemed to want to open her mouth all the way.

She had a small mouth then, Saint Francis asked and laughed.

Very small.

I'm in love with this hoochiemama I'm with right now.

The best relationship I ever had was I bought this redhead a drink then she kissed me and that was it.

Saint Francis laughed.

She's still the prettiest thing I've ever kissed and will ever kiss. It's not like I'm gonna ever lay one on the Mona Lisa, which it's much more unlikely I'll ever stick my dick in her mouth, I don't know, so there's still that, I still have that. I kissed her and that's that.

That is that.

I don't know, the one I want is always the one that doesn't want me.

Yeah.

People always seem to choose Barabbas over me.

Jesus Christ.

I guess it's because I prefer stronger women. It's why I always fall for lesbians and redheads. Is Ashley still around.

No.

You know, I really liked her.

So did everyone else. I think she fucked almost everyone in the house out of the house. Saint Francis put his arm around my shoulder and laughed.

What, I asked. You too.

Well she only sucked my dick.

You fuck, I said and pushed him off of me and we kept walking. I asked him a while later, Did she let you come in her mouth.

He laughed at me. I told her she didn't have to, but she did.

Man. I liked her, but what made her want to spend time with me was what made her not want to spend more time with me. It's just that one that doesn't want me.

You'll grow out of that.

That's too bad, I said and I fell behind Saint Francis to pick another flower. I tore all the petals off at once—she loves me they say she loves me not—and I put the handful in my mouth. I could still see Ashley in my head from the night I was drunk and I walked in on her in the shower when all she did was cover her stomach with her hand and stare at me a second. I stared at her too then I looked her in the eyes and a second later she screamed and I ran out of there.

We crossed another intersection and the houses started to look the same again, but because it was the same street and we were back where we started. Saint Francis and I stood for a while at the bottom of the steps and waited outside for Adam. The car was still there across the street.

Adam says hair makes a woman a woman.

I'm more of a leg man.

Yeah I suppose I sort of am too, though I think I'm more of a where-the-legs-end man.

Saint Francis nodded.

How does your hoochiemama wear her hair.

Short and brown, curly.

Even under her underwear.

She doesn't always wear underwear, but shorter and browner there.

I laughed.

But it's nice to reach out to grab something and feel something there.

A brunette with a body is all you can ever want.

Maybe.

One that can drink as much as you.

She makes me laugh, and she laughs at me. That's all that matters.

I sat down on the second step and put my feet on the first and laid back against the other steps leading to the house. The edge of the step dug into my back. Saint Francis stayed where he stood. My skin itched, so I scratched it and I shut my eyes and the sun was warm and it was red.

Ashley hadn't had the curtain drawn when I walked in on her drunk. She only had her hand on her stomach but covered nothing else, but I couldn't remember what she looked like. I was sitting on the steps in the sun later when she came out and sat down close to me to light a cigarette and I said to her, Ash is Ashing.

Why do you always say that.

I don't know, I like you.

Why do you always say that.

I don't know, I like you.

It's not good to go around telling people you like them. People don't like that.

I thought it might make you like me.

She sighed then said, I do like you.

Can I have some of your cigarette.

She handed it to me and I had a drag then handed it back to her and we sat there and I touched at her elbow and pulled at the skin with my fingertips together like when telling someone to shut their mouth, but then I let go like when kissing the fingertips together then opening them up after tasting something good. I did it again and again like when pretending one's hand was a mouth to speak for someone else.

146

Do you keep touching my elbow because you want to hold my hand.

No, I just like touching you.

Holding my hand is touching me.

I touched her elbow down to her hand then I held her hand with our fingers interlocked.

Ash is Ashing.

You know, I'm just in an emotional state right now where I'm not ready to be with anyone.

I'm not anyone.

Maybe not, but I don't feel like I'm anyone right now either.

I wish I could tell you I could make you feel better, but I can't. Only time can do that. So you know, you should spend some time with me and you'll feel better. I laughed. The speeches I give to myself to give to someone are some of the greatest speeches anyone has ever given to no one. Like, don't miss what's in front of you, looking at what's behind you. Everything takes time.

You're the dumbest smartest person I've ever met.

At least I'm not the smartest dumbest.

You'd be better off, she said and let go of my hand and went back inside.

Saint Francis said he thought he saw Adam down the street some then came and sat down next to me, but I kept my eyes closed and we waited a while without saying anything.

But still, poets get all the pussy, and you know how it is with poets, and that way they have of pronouncing things, like poesy.

It's cause their mouths are always full of poesy, I heard Adam say with his mouth full.

Hey I watered those the other day, don't eat those motherfucks, you motherfuck.

I waited in the car and watched the people going in and out the pharmacy across the street. Adam had backed into the spot and I told him to leave the car running then moved over to sit behind the wheel and adjust the rearview mirror to watch him and Saint Francis walking to the supermarket until I couldn't see them anymore.

I had told Adam, No one suspects a man in a suit.

I'd rather be inconspicuous.

Which is why they'll watch you but not think you'd be so stupid to pull some shit in a suit.

Do you want me to buy the beer, Saint Francis asked me.

I already gave him the money.

What are you even gonna steal then.

I'll find something, Adam said.

Bananas.

It'll be fine, Saint Francis said.

Maybe. I don't know. I already have a record.

They don't even do anything if they catch you. They just don't let you back in again. They just call you sir and grab you and walk you into a small room to sit down and take your picture and tell you to leave and not come back.

How do you know.

They took a picture of me in the one on the other side of campus. It isn't that bad.

You fucker, Adam had said and they got out and walked across the lot until they disappeared.

There was a woman in tight black shorts crossing the street but I couldn't tell how old she was with her back to me, though she must have been a mother. I was sad the lot for the pharmacy was much shorter than the lot for the supermarket. I tried not to think about driving, but if the two of them came running and someone came running after them I would then have to pull out of where we were parked with all the other cars lined up at an angle along the small street between the two lots then I would make a quick right at the light and drive, but then again I didn't even know how to drive stick shift. It had been more than enough time for the two of them to get in and get out.

I leaned across the seat to open the dashboard, but the bottle wasn't there anymore, though the Bible was and there was a redheaded pack of cigarettes too. Adam's mother used to smoke and Adam told me she smoked reds, but that was a while ago. The pack had been flattened out under the hardcover Bible. Andrea smoked the same sort of cigarettes when I drove her home the one time. I slid one out and smelled the cigarette and it smelled like caramel. Andrea smelled like cigarettes. She was bent over—the bend sinister they say the bends dexter—and went up and down while I drove and my dick crooked to the right went straight into her mouth. I took out the white lighter from my jacket and put the pack in my other pocket before I lit one and it was stale. Her forehead was acned with a dozen red spots and she must have been thirteen or fourteen. She was her red hair and her red forehead. I inhaled the cigarette again and I had a tickle in my throat—cough they say laugh—and I coughed and I wondered if some of the older children sitting outside the pharmacy were laughing at me, no, they were too far away to see me. She was wet when I fingered her enough that she left a small stain on the passenger seat that never did come out, but a few years later I sold the car to some kid down the street for more than what it was worth.

My skin itched and I tried not to scratch. I heard them laughing and looked back and saw they were at the sides of the car. I opened the door and put out the cigarette then got out and there was Saint Francis empty-handed and Adam struggling with a case of beer, Adam in his suit, Saint Francis in a pair of overalls he said he had made himself and he wore over a plain white shirt he borrowed from someone in the house because he lost his shirt sometime last night. It was tight on him. Adam handed me the beer and I asked them,

How was the free market capitalism.

There's no such thing as capitalism, Saint Francis said.

I think you just did it.

We just did capitalism, Adam said. Steal from the rich and give to the poor.

Steal from the poor and give to the reich, Saint Francis said.

It just so happens that we're the poor. I sat the case down with me in the backseat and tore the top open to look at the sparkling red and silver and blue. I opened one to drink that was cold and good. Which is better because there's no middle man, the reason why capitalism doesn't and does work, the middle man. I had half of the beer in the time it took them to decide who was going to drive and it was Saint Francis because he knew where we were headed to go up into the hills and Adam was tired of driving. They got in and I asked Adam, Where's the change for the beer.

It came out even.

Everything's fuckin highway robbery these days.

He turned back to me, Hey man I was the one sticking my neck out. There's a cost of living.

There's always a middle man.

Let's just go before it gets dark.

Did you get anything, I asked Saint Francis.

No, I was running interference.

Saint Francis eased out of the spot and took a right at the light. He made something of a living off of unemployment, but I had never seen him work, which made sense when thinking about it, though unemployment was nothing for someone to live off of if it wasn't subsidized from time to time by theft. He drove us up toward the hills behind the Berkeley campus while Adam pulled the chair back some and put his hands down his pants and pulled out a small jar filled with brine and some sort of flesh.

What happened to your diet, I asked him.

It doesn't count stolen goods.

That's good.

And it's pickled herring, Saint Francis said. It's practically raw.

Adam opened the jar and the car filled with the fish smell and we rolled down our windows as he offered us some and I held up my hand no, but Saint Francis went ahead as Adam scooped the small pieces into his hand in between ones for himself. He went on about the amanitas as I drank. I moved the beer case off the seat and stretched my legs behind Adam's headrest and out the window then reached for a second one.

You sure you don't want one, Adam asked me.

Alright, sure. I'll try one.

Adam passed the jar back to me as I tried not to think of it being down his pants. I offered him a beer and he waved it off while he went through his pockets. I pulled my feet in and sat up again to hold the beer between my legs while I had some of the herring and it tasted like it was smoked and the brine stuck to my hand after I tried to wipe it off on my pants. I passed it back to Adam a while later after he had started on the first of several apples.

It didn't take too long to get into the hills east of the city where the road shrank and steepened and all the houses were larger and everything became greener with the altitude, where Angel told me his father worked and the nuclear facilities were, but where the ones who worked there said they weren't. There was no way to tell the truth. The air was thick there. The hills were green and the road was thin winding its two lanes back and forth through the trees and farther still toward the mountains. It must have rained hard not too long ago the way the air went straight into my lungs and was too much for me that I rolled my window up until it was cracked open an inch and still it went to my head but felt good.

Adam tossed an apple core to the side of the road where

the trees were growing up against the pavement as their roots reached to make the road seem thinner than it was. He started on another small apple, so I downed a beer to start on another one too. I offered him a can that he waved off again just as Saint Francis reached back and I opened one for him and we drank. Adam struggled to reach for something that had slid down the front of his pants and even farther down to his pant leg, unbuckling his belt and pulling whatever it was back up again. Saint Francis swerved the car and Adam hit his head on the half down window and let out a fuck as we laughed at him.

Take a look at this hoochiemama, Adam said feeling his head and trumpeting a brown butcher paper wrapped cut of some sort of meat while the wind blew the smell of fish.

What is it, I asked.

Wild caught salmon.

You're really playing fast and loose with the fruits.

What do you mean, salmon is the fruit of the sea.

What about sea cucumbers, Saint Francis said.

Are cucumbers a fruit.

Not if they're pickled.

What about pickled herring, I asked. The pickle of the sea.

Isn't herring a freshwater fish.

It tasted pretty salty to me.

Adam unraveled the wrapping and said, I don't know but this was fourteen dollars a pound.

Jesus fuck. Sometimes I wonder why money costs so much.

Well, it was marked down from seventeen a pound.

That's not too bad then, how much did you get.

A pound.

He saved three dollars.

More or less.

How're we eating it.

Raw, Adam said when he unwrapped it and took a bite.

Raw and red, Saint Francis said.

Adam ate some and passed it to me and there were several mouthfuls missing with teethmarks where he had bitten into it and I started at the other end and I took a bite and drank it down with a bit of beer and it wasn't bad.

It's good, I said and handed the pound or so back to Adam who then passed it to Saint Francis and the fish went back and forth between them until they finished it and Adam threw it out of the window and we drove deeper into the woods. Saint Francis and I had another pair of beers while Adam said to look out for any pined and needled trees. We looked for them, but I closed my eyes from time to time while I drank.

There's supposed to be this nuclear research facility somewhere around here, I said.

Is there.

I wonder how that'll affect the mushrooms.

Probably on some anatomic level, make the mushrooms cloudy and what not.

Did you know they say shamans would consume the mushroom then piss for everyone else to drink their piss because the urine is what contains the most purified high.

Adam and Saint Francis talked and I put my legs up again and remembered the first time I had a drink when I was twelve and they said it would taste like piss, but it was good and I pretended I didn't like it. I closed my eyes and decided to get piss drunk and wander around the woods. There would be all sorts of places to piss.

Saint Francis pulled to the side of the road where there was a ditch with room for us to get out of the car then walk up into a field with a number of pines. Adam must have been halfway across the field by the time Saint Francis and I finished our beers and got out and he turned to me with a handful of pink ovoid pills. One of the three was turned over and had a cervical separation down the middle. Saint Francis called after Adam, Do you wanna do some drugs. Adam might not have heard him or wanted any and he kept going through the field until he reached the handful of trees then disappeared under one. Saint Francis turned back to me and said, I think I'll have some then. Do you want some.

I don't know, maybe I should try to get off the pills.

What do you mean.

I had a near-death experience. They're too much of a certainty for me. I don't like the dosages.

Saint Francis frowned at his palm then up at me.

You know what they say, I said. No pills a day keeps the doctors away.

These are hardly the pills they talk about, he said as he put one of them down on the hood and went through his wallet and found a university card that belonged to someone who didn't look at all like him. He crushed the pill and started to cut it into a thick line.

What are they.

Anti-gravity pills.

But I have a fear of flying.

These help with that.

Alright, doctor. I do think I might be suffering from too much gravitas.

He smiled an uneven grin and separated the pink powder into two lines. One for you, one for me, none for Adam.

Right, I don't think Adam's the snorting type.

It's just Xanax.

The least we could do is one for him too then.

Yeah, Saint Francis said and he dug out the pills again and handed me one and he went for his beer with his pill and I went for mine to drink them down together. One for you, one for me.

We stood there for a second, the pink pill in one hand and the drink in the other.

This is the flesh, I said. This is the blood.

Flesh and blood, he said and we had them and he went back to cutting the lines.

Popping pills and drinking alcohol together, as opposed to just popping pills, is like the difference between transubstantiation and just popping pills. I drank some more beer as I went through my pockets then asked him, Do you have a dollar.

He looked through his wallet again and gave me one so I rolled it up tight then handed it back to him when all the powder had been divided into two lines. He snorted a line and held his nostril shut when he gave me the dollar again. I had mine and didn't feel much but didn't mind.

Shall we, he asked.

Let me get another beer, I said and downed mine and threw the can across the road.

Get me one too, he said and did the same.

Adam had disappeared somewhere in the trees. We could see from the side of the road that the branches came down around the trunks and low enough to the ground that he had to bend over to go under the leaves and see if there were amanitas sprouting around the roots. We left the road to cut across the ditch and go into the field with tall yellow grass broken up every so often by a tree. Saint Francis walked ahead of me to where the hill steepened and the tallest grass came up to the tops of our legs. We could see where it had been stepped through before to go up to the trees, but it wasn't Adam and it might have been stepped through a long time before we got there.

All I heard was the grass bending under our feet then springing back some while Saint Francis breathed heavily until he stopped to drink and look around. I passed by him and went for a tree to crouch under it and look at its roots and found nothing, going out the other side and coming back around, but Saint Francis had started off in another direction. I drank and couldn't see Adam then I decided to go farther up the hill.

The day before New Year's Eve and the day before I met

up with Adam was when I was in the middle of the beginning of a good bender and I met a redhead that evening in the second or third bar and went with her to the third or fourth, which was the hardest one to remember. The two of us were away from the counter and the other couches and on a brown leather one near the end with some tears in the cushions pushing the dirtied yellow plush out, but she didn't mind with her legs up in my lap and an imported beer in her hand. I felt the stubble at the bottoms of her thighs, not quite fully formed hairs, but still a prickly pair of legs.

She was redheaded and freckled and we had been talking about something before she put her legs in my lap, before I had to try hard not to look up her jean skirt or see down her black blouse since she had the biggest and brownest but almost black eyes and she would see everything I did. We had been talking about where she was from.

It's all sixteen year olds going into the woods on LSD, she said. Or going shooting.

I knew you were the Big Bad West Virginia Wolf.

She squinted at me and her eyes were normal sized.

What great big eyes you have, I said. I knew there was something else I liked about you.

Something else huh, she asked. She looked like she had just turned three years old, but I didn't want to ask. I like being liked, she said. Tell me something else.

I rather like girls with southern accents.

You like southern girls.

Yeah, if they have southern accents. Yours isn't quite as deep though is it.

Ain't it.

The next few trees wouldn't reach as low to the ground but still looked skirted by their needles and I still had to bend down to get to their trunks and take a look around, brushing away some of the browner needles and smaller branches that had fallen to mulch. I went through them like that. There was always nothing and I would come out the other side and go to the next one that was a dozen or more feet away, keeping my head down until I was near the end of the beer and I had to tilt my head back to drink some and stare at the blue-gray sky. Looking ahead again I saw Adam farther up the hill than I was. He was going for a few trees clustered closer together. I looked back and saw Saint Francis going toward the way we had been driving up, maybe back to the car, maybe to get another beer.

Get me one too, I yelled but he kept walking downhill.

The redhead crushed several pills against the porcelain sink and ground them under a card as I fingered through the twenties in a white envelope for one that felt crisp to roll and reroll, waiting for her to finish cutting the pink dust at the edge of the sink. The bathroom was a tight fit for the two of us and it must have once been tiled, but it was now covered in penises and people writing that they were there. I stood against the back of the door and didn't bother to look anymore.

What great big eyes you have, I said. What pretty little pink pills you have.

You ain't afraid of me are you Little Red Riding Hood.

Well not that little. But everything must look so little to you cause you have the biggest eyes I've ever seen. I think I can see my life and death in them.

She stopped cutting the lines and looked at me until I could see everything in them that might disappear if they were to close. Tell me something else, she said.

Something else I like about you.

You're making me blush.

I like that you do the drugs.

Do you do the drugs.

Sometimes yeah, when it's warm I like to do the drugs. I'm more of a fair weather fiend.

I'm sure you are.

Ajax, I asked with the twenty between my thumb and forefinger like a joint.

She squinted at me and grabbed the bill and put her head down to the lines, pressing on a nose ring I hadn't noticed, though most of her features were lost on me to her eyes. She was redheaded and freckled though. She snorted her line and handed me back the twenty and I tightened it again and we slid past each other to end up where the other stood. She had a finger covering one nostril as she still smelled it with her eyes closed.

Even if we didn't find anything I wouldn't have minded us driving farther into the woods and pulling to the side of the road again. Nature was repetition—so as above so below they say so as lo and behold—but we were always too close or too far away to see that. I finished the beer and felt good enough to throw the empty can away into the tall grass. I wanted to leave some mark on the woods that was more than just pissing on a tree, even if it was the tree of life. Maybe that was the reason for all of the differences between men and women. Men could piss standing up, so they went around pissing on everything. There was a handful of trees toward the car in between the ones I had gone through, the ones Adam passed, the ones Saint Francis hadn't bothered with, the ones in the middle of it all. I headed down the slope where the dirt had turned to mud, slipping forward because of my dress shoes while holding onto some of the thicker grass to not fall down.

I came to the first tree and went under to have the same look around for nothing before going out the other end to move onto the next tree for the same nothing and onto the next nothing when I saw a dirtied blanket covering something tucked against the trunk. There was some clothing at the side and it all looked like it had been left there for a long time but for some reason. I ran out from under the tree and climbed up the slope and farther up to a clearing to look for the others. I went down the hill again and slipped and fell on my ass hard then I stood up, wiping myself off on the grass while yelling out to them how I found something.

Where are you, I heard Adam from farther up the hill.

Over here.

What.

Polo.

Marco, Saint Francis yelled from down the hill and he sounded closer than Adam.

Polo, Adam yelled from above me.

Marco, I yelled.

Polo.

Marco.

Polo, I yelled back and started slowly toward the tree again. Polo.

Hey you motherfuck, Saint Francis said and I saw him down the hill some with beer in hand.

I found something that belongs to someone.

What.

Marco, Adam yelled.

I'm not sure what it is, I said. Watch out for the mud.

Polo.

Did you go back for another beer, I asked.

No, Saint Francis said as he climbed to where I was and I gave him a hand and he let go of the can and it rolled down the slope. Did you.

No.

Marco.

Polo, Saint Francis and I yelled in unison until Adam showed up at the side of the clearing but halfway up the slope. He took his time coming down, so Saint Francis and I went ahead to go see what it was. I pulled the blanket away from the box it covered, which had a yellow gourd molded over next to a coconut and a stack of papers that had been wetted together.

What in the fuck.

Did you find something, Adam said once he was under the tree.

No, Saint Francis said. I don't think so.

I started thumbing through the pages that almost tore with the ink bleeding through, but it still seemed like it was something more than what it was. It was in Spanish and handwritten and hard to read. The pages I could peel apart were the same handful of sentences repeated again one after the other, all of them starting the same way.

Todos los árboles, I said. Todos los árboles. I handed a page to Saint Francis. All the trees.

Yeah, all the trees. I'm not sure what else though. It's all bled out.

Why would they leave this here.

He looked at it for a while but couldn't make any more sense of it then he said, I don't know.

This coconut isn't bad, Adam said. Feel the hairs on it.

I felt the brown hairs and said, Maybe we should go.

Yeah I could use a drink.

Me too.

Adam took the coconut when we left to go slowly down the slope, through the clearing and to cross the ditch again, saying something about trying some more trees down the road. Saint Francis said he didn't mind driving and I wondered if he had anymore Xanax.

I pinched my nose and smelled it and the redhead watched me.

You aren't afraid of me are you, she asked.

No.

You should be.

I am.

Don't be afraid.

I'm not. I think you're a sheep in wolf's clothing.

She finished cutting up another pair of lines and we snorted them.

Do you feel anti-depressed, I asked.

I do feel anti-depressed.

You look pretty anti-depressed. You look pretty pretty.

You're not so bad yourself.

Pretty pretty, huh.

Pretty pretty, pretty anti-depressed.

I looked at her brownish black or blackish brown eyes and felt good. I kissed her neck and bit her earlobe and pressed her head down and I tried not to look at her looking up at me.

You're not wearing any underwear Little Red Riding Hood.

No, all the times I've ever had to take my pants off, I've never been all that happy about those extra few seconds it took to take my underwear off too.

She went back and forth as I thought of nothing else until she went to wash her mouth and she sat down to piss and I was afraid so I pulled up my pants and got out of there and closed the door behind me then leaned my back against it before I went to the counter to have one for the road.

When we got to the side of the road Adam threw the coconut against the concrete and cracked the coconut open and it burst into dozens of pieces along the road, him and Saint Francis running after the largest chunk. They said Andrea wasn't driving but she died the second the car wrapped around the tree. We walked around picking up the pieces of coconut that had sprung farther than the others, scraping with our teeth all the good white flesh onto our tongues.

What a voice Andrea had though, warm and almost like my own.

Adam fell asleep with his mouth open and he sounded like he was choking while we drove down the hills, but in the end of the afternoon when we got to the house and I woke him he got up to go inside to the couch and he took his jacket off then he curled up under it to fall asleep again. Saint Francis brought the leftover beer to the workbench and we started drinking again while he messed with a lighter, blackening the edges of the beige table to burn the pressed wood to look less fake, lacking the tree rings for us to count how old it was, but it aged several centuries in the few seconds I drank and watched.

How're the Xanax treating you, he asked me.

I don't know. How am I supposed to feel.

Like you don't know.

That's good I guess.

Adam started snoring again, so we went outside and brought the few beers left in the case to the top step of the stairs and sat down and we started to start drinking again. We said nothing for a while in the sun and I couldn't think of what to think of other than the top step being the nicest to sit on in the sun when the wood was warmed from the afternoon. The day wasn't too windy too often and wasn't too bad when it was. The time went by slowly but enough for me to wish the day would be as long and as good as the afternoon.

I'm gonna go to a poetry reading with Anna if you wanna come.

I have to go to see Allison. I told her yesterday I wanted to see her and she just asked me if I was here again and I said no.

Does she know you're here now.

I don't know.

What time are you going.

I don't know. Soon, I think.

Okay.

What time is the reading.

Later probably.

Yeah, alright. I thought poetry was dead.

There'll be something to drink there.

Long live poetry, I said and we finished our beers and started on new ones. I seem to meet the same woman every time I drink.

Then keep drinking.

We drank and I said, That's what she always tells me.

Who's she.

Lady liquor.

Motherfuck. What're you doing tomorrow.

I'm going to go see this girl Eve.

Eve.

Yeah, I haven't seen her in a year, but I'm in love with her. It was the last time I came up from Los Angeles. Motherfuck man, I miss her already. She has synesthesia, you know, but when we met she asked me when I was born and seemed to have an orgasm right at that moment, cause she likes the number three, it's her synesthesiac number or whatever, or one of them.

The number three is everyone's synesthesiac number.

I thought that too. The number three is red for her but then it's like sight and sound is the same difference for her too. She likes me that I'm made mostly of threes or derivatives of threes. I even memorized her birthday and height and everything to see how she does, but it doesn't make much of a difference for me.

That's nice of you to do.

Though I do always tell her that I eight her. Like, eight instead of hate. I always tell her I eight you, I eight you, I eight you, I eight you. It's how I tell her how I love her. Because she was born on the eighth of the eighth of the eighty-eighth. I eight that she was born.

Yeah, a lot of times you say I hate you to say I love you.

We drank until I lost track of whose turn it was to talk, but

I would still laugh before and after everything we said, so it didn't make a difference. Why are we always talking about girls, I asked him. What are we, boys.

I don't know, what else is there.

What do men talk about.

Women.

Not always.

Love.

Everyone wants to be loved for who they aren't.

Love, be loved. There's nothing else.

All you need is who you love to love you.

That isn't love.

No, but it's everything. Love is kind of everything.

Love is the fear of losing love.

Love is love.

I think it's the first sight that I love more than the love itself.

That's not love.

Yeah but a beautiful woman you see the first time is. Looks are everything. See anyone can be born intelligent, but not everyone can be born beautiful, besides, intelligence fades, dementia and what not.

What even is beauty.

They say it's symmetry.

Models though, if you think about them.

I do.

They're never really beautiful, they're all just sort of ugly in a good way.

For supermodels it's supersymmetry.

Tall dark and then some, Saint Francis said and he laughed at himself.

There was still some sun we were sitting in, but it had gotten cold and Saint Francis went into the house and came back outside about a beer later with his overalls half down and a buttoned up denim shirt that he had told me he hand

164

stitched the red and pink and white flowers with the long green stems from different materials into the shirt. The stems running up and down the length of his chest left the flowers facing each other around his collar when it was buttoned up all the way, waiting to bloom when he unbuttoned the shirt to give off the stench of sweat and hard drinking. He had made cocktails and brought them out with him and we sipped them because it was colder but still good weather to sit and not do too much. It was just bourbon in the beer, but it burned. I itched and I scratched.

So why'd you come up here.

I'm finding every woman that ever sucked my cock.

He laughed and asked me, Why.

I don't know. I'm grieving. And I like having my cock sucked.

What're you grieving.

This strawberry redhead.

Strawberry blonde.

No, not her. She wasn't. A real firecracker. I don't even remember what she looked like. Now I see any redhead and it reminds me of her.

Well at least she wasn't a blonde or brunette, there's more of them.

Blondes and brunettes remind me of redheads.

Yeah.

She gave me head.

Nice.

Just the one time.

Oral sex is the same as oral contraception.

Yeah, it's why I like big eyes.

What was her name.

*An*drea.

*An*drea.

Yeah, she was a singer or something.

That's too bad, man.

I know, I said and I drank for a while. I like a real manic depressive dream girl.

Saint Francis frowned and said, The whole world is bipolar.

But it feels nice to hold things when they're not too heavy.

You shouldn't mind if they're heavy or not.

Yeah.

Yeah, I also think I'm happier when I'm depressed.

I'd rather my friends be happy than me, cause then they can cheer me up when I'm sad.

Friends are strangers you make excuses for.

What is that.

You're gonna hurt a lot of people and you're gonna hurt a lot.

Then what.

You grow older and you know less people, so you hurt less people.

There's no such thing as friends, only drinking buddies.

So I suppose now we're just experiencing one of the only two emotions, depressed or drunk.

Most of the time it's the two of them together.

Which is depressing.

Yeah, I could use a drink.

We drank.

So what about Adam, Saint Francis asked me.

He's good. He's not good all the time, but even when he's not good, he's not that bad.

Yeah, he seems alright.

His girlfriend, you know, gave me head.

Is that right.

Yeah.

You don't make mistakes because you made mistakes.

I don't know, I think it was because she was older than me. I like older women. Being with an older woman is the same as being with a younger girl. They're almost broken up now though.

A good woman is hard to lose.

You can say that again, my good man. I downed my bourbon and beer to start on another one.

Yeah.

There's all this something you tell someone between a few beers and another few beers, something you always forget about, something you're trying to forget, someone.

What is it.

I forget. No, I'm kidding. I don't know. I was losing my head for a while. Madness is knowing something else no one else does, while genius is dumbing oneself down until everyone does. But there is this fine line somewhere between inspiration and insanity, so I was going around saying I was sick in the head, now that's really somewhat deluded, don't you think, so it doesn't help to be sick in the head, but it doesn't hurt to think that you are. But then again you start to see the repetitions and the patterns and you still have to say something to someone else even if you know they don't exist. That life is pattern. Life is a myth about death. Yeah, I know, but I don't know. I don't want to go to the memorial. The memoralable. The memorioral. Why would I want to go. There's no reason for me. I want to be immortal. Immortality is immorality. I want to be a Greek god, not a Roman sculpture of a Greek god. I want to be Michelangelo and Michelangelo's David. I mean, I don't wanna die. I want to be Dionysus. So yeah I didn't know her that well, but if I did and she died, I would have been broken up by it. She did die several days ago and it did kill me. She died four days ago today. Three days before New Year's Eve. What timing. Four is the new three. She sang something for me after I came in her mouth. I don't know what it was, you know, but I hear it still in my head.

Saint Francis said nothing, but I heard her—sing they say song—in my head.

This might be bad, so it might be good. But all I can do is put all the love I have into this and maybe when I'm dead, maybe not, but maybe then my love will be inside someone and they will feel me inside them and they'll feel loved and they'll love me and they'll love. I don't know, nada. I should head out soon.

The afternoon had turned to evening and I looked at Saint Francis and his chin in his hand and his hand on his knee, half asleep. I shook him from the shoulder and his head fell out of his hand and I helped him up and moved him slowly back to the porch couch. I went in and took the bottle of bourbon—brown they say burn—and I drank some then went outside and back down the steps to the sidewalk and drank again—auburn they say I burn—and I wanted to burn everything I had ever done. I went into the street and looked back and forth and saw both ends of the street looked the same.

I didn't know whose idea it was to photograph a nude calendar for the food collective, maybe one of them talking with their mouths full, but then again I didn't know anyone there other than a tall, thin, blonde-haired brunette, Allison. She said she hadn't seen me in so long when she invited me over for dinner that I could hang around there for a while if I wanted to, but when I got there she said she had something to do the rest of the night.

Most of them had gone upstairs to change when she leaned into me. She didn't really hug me, but she smelled nice saying how good it was to see me again, how I should talk to some of them sitting at the table and how nice they were. She hadn't finished eating but went upstairs too, so I took all of what was left on her plate and spooned it onto mine, finishing the rest of their organic and what they said was not just local but homegrown fare. It wasn't bad.

Allison had asked me when I got there, Did you bring anything.

No, I finished it on the way here. I stood in the doorway. Sorry, was I supposed to.

You didn't have to, but it would've been nice if you did.

Would you even really drink bourbon, I asked once she let me in.

It is dinner.

I remembered the last time I had seen Allison was sometime before she had moved in with the food collective, still living in a building she had moved into with several friends, but by the time I was spending some nights there, she had the apartment to herself. It was always the last times I thought of because it might as well have been the firsts. Her bed was white and she was pale red. She had rolled over onto her side in the time I went to go piss. I stood over her, the bed bug bites itching and me scratching them until they looked like sores and looked worse than they were, but some bites were worse, bruised black and blue from her biting me the night before. I sat down at the end of her bed, which took most of me to not fall over again and crawl up against her—good night they say sleep tight—to fall asleep forgetting the dozen bites that would come with it.

She rolled over and asked me, When's the last time you got laid.

Last night.

That doesn't count.

Why not.

I got laid two days ago.

I'm not too good with days.

The night before last night.

Why're you telling me that.

I thought you should know.

I don't wanna know.

Why not.

You're a pretty woman, it isn't hard for you to get laid. All you have to do is spread your legs. Sometimes you don't even have to.

Oh, you think I'm pretty.

I think you're all woman. I think you're all women.

It wouldn't be hard for you to get laid if you didn't drink so much.

Or if I was a woman.

Especially not if you drank the same as much as you do now.

It doesn't matter how hard my dick gets if it isn't that big.

Do you not think you have a big dick.

No.

You have a big dick, she said and put a hand on me. I should know.

Is it because yours is smaller.

Mine is so small you can't even see it.

What difference does it make if it's big if it still looks small to me.

Would you rather you think it was big but it wasn't.

I don't know. I might be better off not getting you off.

She rolled over again and was tall and thin and went by Alice then. Alice was short for Allison and too short for Alice. Allisons aren't always tall, but most of them are and Alice was too.

Alice an Alice an Alice an Alice.

Yes, that's my names.

It was too hot to sleep the day away without having had already drank most of it anyway. Her back was bare and she was pale where she wasn't freckled, red where she hadn't been bitten, but she was bitten all over and there were older bites still on her skin, purpling like ash like they had been burnt into her flesh like put-out cigarettes.

Did you want a rollie-pollie, she had asked me while she licked the length of the cigarette and we sat on the step and waited for the moon to turn blue the night before. She had rolled a handful of rollie-pollies, so there were some leftover the morning after—DDT is good they say for me-e-e—and I took one. I found my pants on the floor with one of the legs inside out and put them on, left her in bed then started outside and left the door on the hinge enough to get back in. I walked down the hall and saw there was a tic-tac-toe-paned window in the hallway door at the end that I could see in the bottom three panes the letters *o n e* spelled out in red. Alice had told me she used to dye her hair much more when she was younger, which I could tell it had been dyed enough because it was short and reddish brown but darker brown at the roots where it wasn't dead.

So how do you know Allison, someone across the table asked me like I was staring down at my plate for too long.

Ah, you know.

He waited for me to go on then said, Yeah.

I didn't know what he meant so I said to him, We grew up together.

Oh, nice.

I hadn't looked up much because the walk there was long and had left my head to spin and my stomach empty, so I kept my head down and ate and tried to feel better.

Whereabouts, he asked me.

Los Angeles.

She never told me she's from Los Angeles.

Yeah, Los Angeles. Hard *g*.

Well, you must have a lot of stories.

Yeah she does too. She's a real firecracker.

He laughed and I didn't like it and he asked me, How long do you think you'll stay.

Just for dinner. I didn't want to not see Allison.

The rest of them at the table talked around me the way they went on about who would want to pose with what, what month it would have to be for the fruit or the vegetable to be in season. My skin itched and I wondered if it was bed bugs and if that would keep me out of Allison's bed or if she would think it nice of me to bring something. Dinner could always just be dinner, so I ate.

So what brings you up here then.

I'm looking for the tree of life.

He laughed and said, You came to the right place. So what do you do.

I put my fork down with whatever sort of tomato I was eating still forked as I looked up at him and saw he had to have been several years younger than everyone else there. He was blond like a child. I don't know, I said. I drink and I do a lot of drugs.

Really, he asked.

No, I laughed. That's a lie.

He smiled. That's good.

I'm a poet.

Oh, I write some poetry too.

Yeah, but what do you do.

Well, this. I guess. We're called the Conscious Collective.

Why not the Conscience Collective.

Some of the others said something and I couldn't hear him until he repeated himself. There was another collective that already had that name.

What about the Collective Conscience then.

That's not bad either, but it's sort of the same.

Maybe. You could call it CC for short though.

Most of them had finished eating by then and got up to move all of their gourds and stalks and melons and other sorts of decorative fare, taking them from where some were arranged and some left on the dining room table only to be moved to the front room. They went back and forth from the dining room into the front room with their hands full to be emptied again and when I finished with my plate I did the same. I took the mason jar Allison had been sharing with me and filled up again from one of the white wine bottles. It was cheap and good and at least they knew wine was better when it was more expensive but best when it was cheapest. The women were still upstairs to change, most of the men having left for the front room. I took a crookneck squash by its neck and fell in line with them.

The room was large and airy and it had been opened up with all the mismatched furniture and the couches and chairs picked up from the sides of streets around there pushed to the sides of the room. It felt wooden and that made the room feel older and warm and darker than it really was to give the appearance of a main showroom at the sort of house that had other sorts of things going on upstairs. I left the squash with all the other calendar pieces put on a large wooden cable spool sitting on its side as a table at the center of the room. Some of the others went back and forth still but were coming to the front room again empty-handed, looking as though they were trying to do something, so I did the same and I worked on the jar of wine.

You gotta excuse my brother Evan, one of them said and patted me on the shoulder. I think he has something of a thing for Allison.

I couldn't tell.

He stared at me and said nothing.

It's good to have a thing for someone. Good for him. Someone like Allison.

He said his name was Aaron and he looked like he was the head of the collective, so I thanked him for dinner, but he said not to thank him. He smelled bad. You know a lot of vegetarians put on weight.

Is that right.

But I think it's because we've got so many great chefs here.

Ah, right.

He was redheaded and freckled and he stuck out his right hand which was callused as much as his skin was sun-worn and cracked-white. I shook it then he said, Allison's not that great with the introductions.

Yeah, no. You have to get to know her first.

There were a dozen of them there, though the only one that looked like he was supposed to be was the one with the camera, but he was about as bored as the rest of them and he went in circles around the spool taking pictures of the fruits and vegetables, staring into the camera before going several more times around the spool, asking someone to hold something, which gave them something to do. Aaron pointed out who each of them were, each of them looking up when they heard their names and I would nod at them if they said something, knowing I wouldn't remember them by the time Aaron got to the end of the circle we had turned into.

We can't only have the girls be in it, one of them said. He held onto a paper with all the names of the months and fruits and vegetables and some women, running a hand through his brown and curled hair then against his tanned skin before covering one of his green eyes, still looking at the paper.

Because then no girls would buy it and that's like half of our audience right there.

Some of them said something.

So I'll put myself down for whatever month if someone wants to do the same, the one with the paper said. He was wearing a large and white and wooly sweater, too thick with sleeves that were too long. The sweater must have been knit for someone else only to be handed down to him. Well it's not gonna happen if we don't do anything.

Fuck it alright then, another one said. He took off his shirt and he was mostly ribs and hairless and pale, making a show of himself while the others laughed. Let's fuckin do it.

What month do you wanna do.

October, my birthday's in October.

The one with the paper wrote it down and soon enough everyone else was buzzing around and

every time he had to write something he would push the sweater sleeves up again and by the time he finished writing it they would come back down around his wrists and start for his hands just to be pushed up to his elbows again.

I finished the little left over in the mason jar and left for the dining room to get something else to drink while the rest of them put their names with months and women and things they ate, not always in those months, though all of them with their reasons for putting their names with those things, until they had enough for their calendar. There were only bottles of white wine, so I filled up the jar again and drank and started back for the front room when Aaron came up to me again and he looked like he wanted to talk. He poured himself a drink and I patted him on the shoulder and asked him, So what's it all about then.

What's what all about.

The Collective Conscience.

The Conscious Collective.

Yeah, that one.

I think it starts with wanting to eat all the right things, all the things that're good for us that we are supposed to be eating, but along with that it's important to be living off the land. It's not just a thing like how the food tastes when it tastes good, it's more than that, it's also being connected to the nature of it, being a part of it all. Being sure when you feed yourself and feed others, which is what we're doing, when you know all the things you're consuming, that all of it is good, good for you, and just good for everyone.

I nodded with his cadence.

For me, I don't understand this obsession with consumption, with overconsumption. There's a reason consumption used to be the name of a disease, and it still is, I would say. It's because how sickening consumption is. It's the reason why here we're all so interested in understanding what it is we're consuming, what we're putting in our bodies, making sure it's good for us.

That's good.

People don't want quantity, they want quality.

Right, I want more quality. I know what you mean.

I really think you do.

I wondered where all the naked women were and I asked him, Where do you think that comes from though.

I would say the feeling in part comes from the release of endorphins, the feeling you get from working with your hands, that feeling of dirt and the earth on your hands, but then I mean, really it's all about sowing seeds and reaping what you sow.

You know they say seeding creation is seeing creation.

I never heard that, that's lovely. You know, you really are a poet.

Well, thanks man. I drank and I felt good.

That's the idea, there's this understanding you get from the seasons, about timeliness, as in the reality of birth and rebirth, creation and recreation, like, we'll go on doing what we're doing, and we'll go on.

Right. I drank while he went on and I felt better than good.

So what do you think.

I think everything. I drank and said, I think everything you can think of. Everything comes in fractals, everything in the universe and everything you could see and everything in between. Say trees for instance, some of the most clear fractals to see the fractals in, all their branches, all their leaves and their stems, all the limbs and even the roots and the trunk, all of it similar, everything is to everything else because everything is everything.

Yeah, man. That's what that is. He squinted until it looked like his eyes must have been closed and maybe that was how he saw everything.

I tried squinting like him to see whatever it was he was, but I tried too hard and saw nothing. I opened my eyes again and saw him there, his eyes wide, the blood vessels in his reddened eyes. I watched him looking at his hand like a tree with his fingers as branches. I told him, It's like when you think of a single cell in you that can't know what you are in your entirety. You're that cell too in whatever you're in in this entirety.

Did you know it takes ten years for all the cells in the body to replace themselves.

No.

Yeah, you're not who you are ten years ago.

I'm not who I am ten beers ago.

He laughed.

I drank and I told him, This champagne is the worst.

I think it's white wine.

Even worse. White wine is the worst kind of champagne.

He smiled as he asked me, Do you smoke. He made a motion with his thumb and index finger up against his lips and I could see the dirt under his fingernails.

I can, yeah. I forced myself to the end of my drink. I think

I may get some more to drink first.

Yeah of course. Help yourself.

We went back to the other room and I poured the white wine for us and followed him upstairs and past the rooms where the women were doing the sorts of things women did before men saw them naked. We went through one of the upstairs windows out onto the roof over the front room. It was dark and cold outside, so I stayed standing and I walked back and forth.

Watch it out here, Aaron said and he sat down on the dark wooden shingles and started to roll a joint and I drank while I waited.

Yeah, I'm not quite fall down drunk yet. There isn't enough alcohol in this world to get me fall down drunk. At least, not tonight.

The house was up in the Berkeley hills and from where we were I could see the lights from all the streets there and farther down the streets closer to the bay, the lights on the bridges, the lights from the city. Most of the time it was covered up in the fog. It wasn't always like that, but a lot of the time it was, so to see the light from across the bay made me feel as small as the light from the bay must have felt to see the night, though I couldn't make out any other constellations but Orion and even his shoulders seemed small. There weren't many constellations to see, but it wasn't that we couldn't see the night from where we were, it was that it wasn't as good as being farther up in the hills where we could see the light and the night. It wasn't nothing, but nothingness.

I'll roll you a rollie-pollie, Allison had said the night we waited for the moon to turn blue. We spent the night sitting on the steps because she heard they said it would turn blue, that it wouldn't again for another three years, which was a long time. We waited until we could see it well enough, but when it didn't look blue the way they said it would, it was still bright and full and looked the way it was supposed to. The light from the moon didn't let us see many constellations.

In the morning I sat on the steps again and stared at the red *o n e* spelled out in *loading zone*. I looked at the warehouses all along the other side of the street and some more warehouses starting halfway down the side of the street where Allison lived. The sun had been rising for a while and I went through her matches until the rollie-pollie caught on fire, maybe because of the sun, but the end of it went up in smoke then settled when it burned toward the tobacco. The bug bites burned in the sun as I smoked, but it was the only way to get rid of them, fumigating from the inside out. It was a good day to sit in the sun.

The warmth went into my chest and I held my breath and could feel them burning until neither of us could take it anymore and I let go and watched their dying breaths go up in the morning air. I took long drags and felt them crawling around inside my lungs until they were dead as I sat there with my head in my hands and the sun on my back.

I heard something crawling into my ear and remembered hearing all the bigger bugs crawling around in the walls the night before and I scratched at my ear and saw it was Allison. She smiled sitting next to me with a rollie-pollie in her hand. She wore a sundress and all the older bug bites looked like sunspots on her skin and she held the rollie-pollie to her mouth and it trembled in her hand while she leaned toward me and her breath smelled like drinking, but she still smelled nice. It caught fire with our mouths close together and the two rollie-pollies end to end.

Fumar puede matar, she said and she exhaled.

She had a deep voice that came out with her laugh when it wasn't swallowed up by her smile. Her teeth were bright yellow with thick separations between them that would have made her look girlish if she weren't so tall, but her smile fit her face well and was wide as much as her face was wide with strong cheekbones that brought out her green eyes and strawberry freckles.

Fumar puede matar.

She made a truncated cross with her hands together like she was calling for time, but then she broke it in half and spelled out on the top of the cross and the start of her hand, *f u m a r*, only to break it in half the other way and start from the middle of where the top of the cross would have been, spelling it out from where the *m* and the *m* would have matched, *m a t a r*.

Fumar puede matar.

Huh.

To smoke is to kill.

Oh.

I saw that on some wall in España somewhere.

Allison held the back of her hand that spelled matar against my forehead. I might have looked worse than I could see, staring at myself sitting in the sun, so I made the cross too and looked at the redness that had covered my hands in the night. I let go of the cross and I inhaled until my heart went up into my throat then down into my chest and I coughed some of the bugs out, covering my mouth with the hand I had spelled fumar with, feeling her hand on my back, which was soft and cold. I took another breath and my heart went down deeper to the bottom of my stomach, staying there while she scratched me here and there and where I hadn't been bitten. She leaned over and bit me herself then smiled while some of the ashes fell against her legs. She must not have felt anything.

Chain smokers are serial killers, she said.

She laughed and coughed and I put my hand on her back and I tried to remember what I could about her, but there was nothing about some wall in España somewhere. She had told me the first guy she had ever been with always smoked cigarettes that came in bright red cartons, which even sounded the way it would when she was at that age when things were bright and red that came in cartons. She had told me she wanted to sing, but she gave it up and that was why she smoked and why her voice had grown deeper than before.

So what do you think, Aaron said. He finished licking the length of the joint. Shall we.

Yeah, why not. I sat down next to him and drank some wine and it went down like water. This white wine tastes like honey.

He lit the joint and held his breath and didn't say anything as he passed the joint to me then he exhaled and either laughed or coughed.

I set the jar down and held the joint to my lips and I inhaled. With wine it was always a matter of waiting for it to get there, but it was always something else that made one realize the wine was there all along. All one had to do was hold their breath to keep it all where it was and just hope it didn't go somewhere else again. It was nice being there. I would tell Allison that since I now had something to say. I exhaled and saw the smoke go up into the night and there was nothing I could do about that.

Now I did hear marijuana is a gateway drug, Aaron said.

Marijuana is a gateway drug into the fourth dimension, nada.

Nada, he asked.

Yeah, nada.

He laughed as I inhaled and exhaled again then passed the joint back to him.

Though I guess we just live in three and a half dimensions.

How's that.

We're in the present right, but we're always half in the past or the future. Really, we're always in between, maybe we're really three and ninety ninth dimensions, right.

I would say three and one hundredth.

Right, I said and I felt like I had pissed my pants and I stood up to walk back and forth.

Here you go man, he said as he passed the joint to me.

The passed is the past. I laughed and repeated myself and said, Like the past. The passed joint is the past joint. I inhaled and exhaled and handed it back to him then walked back and forth.

You're half in. We're each having half.

Everything is so meta.

Everything is.

We could sum up everything in no more than a few words if we didn't repeat ourselves just to live longer to have something else to say.

A few words lasts a lifetime.

Everything is everything or *a b a*.

He held the joint to his mouth.

When you try to define something though, try to put it into words, it becomes what it is, rather than all the things it isn't. You think without words when you don't have the words for something. I looked up at the night and said, I don't think people look up enough.

No, he said as he was looking up. Here you go man.

He handed me the joint and I sat down next to him and looked at the night again. We're white approaching black. You see the black then you look at the white and you see the black again, but this time it looks sort of gray. If all you think of is the bad, you'll never see the good.

I see what you're saying, but I'm not too good at that.

Sometimes I blink when my eyes are closed. I think it must be muscle memory, or something. I inhaled and exhaled and passed the joint back to him, having neared the end of it and I stood up slow and finished the jar of wine and looked at the night. You can go ahead and kill it.

He held the joint to his mouth and when he exhaled he stood up and tried to hand it to me.

Thanks man, I'm good.

Okay.

He stood there and held what was left of it to his mouth as he stared at the end of his nose.

I watched him and said, I don't think I'll ever learn to French inhale. It's all I've ever wanted to do. That's not true. You know, there are these lies I tell myself when I don't want anyone to know the truth, but I don't know what that is. I finished the jar of wine. The point, you know, what is it.

I don't know man.

What is anything I'm doing.

I think you're doing alright, man. You seem like a good guy.

Fuck it man, when we're as old as we are. I looked at him and wasn't sure how old he was. All we should be looking for are virgins that are still our age. The virgins that haven't been sacrificed to some volcano already, those are the only sure ones there are left for us man. They're the fuckin virgins and I'm the fuckin volcano. They're fuckin Pompeii and I'm fuckin Vesuvius.

Yeah.

We're so close to the end I'd rather just bacchanal until it all collapses.

Yeah.

We're all just holes, man. We're all just holes fucking holes.

Holes or tunnels. Holes are tunnels.

I think I drink to excess a lot though.

It's better to smoke.

I'm too drunk to be high.

What were we talking about.

I don't know. I think the last line I told you was I have a bad memory.

Which line.

Right.

I don't know.

I don't either.

When the white wine and the weed were there with us we

had everything to say, but then as if we hadn't said anything, Aaron put the roach out against a shingle then in his pocket and we went back inside through the window. I felt warm and I followed him down the stairs to get another jar before I left, but there they all were, all of them naked. All the naked women looking like virgins, some of them thin like young boys, some of the others that looked like their mothers or like they could be mothers, some of them in the way some god had left them and some of them in the way men wanted them—Gaia they say Gaius—all the naked men there too, all of them as though they were already sinners covering themselves.

Allison was there and I could see her face in all the other ones I didn't know and all the bodies I didn't know, all the ones that lost their meaning when I saw hers and it wasn't bitten like before but as white as it could be, but I knew it was hers and I knew who she was and I knew her name. I knew they weren't virgins and I wasn't the volcano and I tried not to look at her again.

What if it's all in my head.

What if it isn't.

What if it is that it isn't.

They were all the women, not of my past, but of a future that will never be. They would never look as good as I would remember them, so I tried not to look at any of them, but it was taking a long time for them to get through the year. How thin she was with her red hair and now how she looked almost like a child smiling while the one with the camera walked around her and a blonde and a brunette a few times as they covered themselves in strawberries.

Allison and I had played hot hands, though we didn't play hard because the rollie-pollies were still in our mouths and our hands were already red. She kissed my hands after I let her win and I felt red since I could sort of see my mother's face in her cheekbones if they weren't freckled. Hot hands turned into holding hands then into nothing.

Life isn't that bad when you're holding someone's hand.

A lot of times you have to shake their hand first.

I shook her hand and held on. I looked at my hands and how if it weren't for the bug bites how I couldn't tell them apart other than being opposites. Her hands were the same, though her fingers were a bit crooked.

It's too bad you can't shake your own hand and introduce yourself.

Yeah, too bad.

I rested my head against the warm concrete bannister and tried to remember her dancing some sort of jitterbug the night before.

Do you wanna go get something to drink.

I nodded without opening my eyes but knew she would still be there when I did.

Okay then.

She went upstairs and came back down with one of her shirts she put on me and we walked to the bodega and I asked her, What do you wanna get.

She shrugged and smiled and she said, Beer is bread.

We stood there fumigating for a while in the shade. It was a good day to stand in the shade, so we stayed there and looked at some of the fruits and the vegetables at the front of the bodega and finished our cigarettes. I flicked mine into the street and said to Allison, La cucaracha is Spanish for the jitterbug.

No it isn't.

Immortalidad is Spanish for a cockroach.

I think that's right.

Immortality is a cockroach.

She went inside and said to the man behind the counter, Give us today our daily bread.

I went over and took a carton of strawberries and started down the street to wait for her there. The strawberries were almost cheap enough to feel bad about taking them, but they were red and good and we ate them on the way back and there was only one that was rotten. All the other ones were good and ripe and we threw the green ends into the street until we got back and went inside. The sun was still on our eyes and it was darker than it looked, but we drank the beers and when I could see her teeth again I could see they were stained red.

What do you think, Aaron asked me.

Huh.

I don't feel right looking at them naked and me not being naked.

Oh, yeah. I've been feeling sort of pheromonal as of late.

Yeah.

I felt overdressed as I buttoned up my suit and said to Aaron, No one looks good after they've had dinner.

They do, don't they.

It's odd don't you think the way things work, you always take someone out on a date to dinner then you have sex. You should have sex then take them out to dinner. You look even better while you're having sex and you feel even hungrier while you're eating.

Everything was in the room with them. Everything they had taken out of the earth, everything that might have fallen to the earth if they hadn't plucked them when they had, everything looked bright and ripe and the way it was supposed to look. Everything was there.

Well, I guess I should have come earlier.

He laughed.

I don't know what month it is, I told him. Some of them stood there with their shirts off if they weren't cold. Some of them had changed into thin dresses, wearing nothing under them, though I could still almost see them under their clothes. All of them could be naked in a second if the one with the calendar told them it was their turn.

I wouldn't remember their names and soon enough I

would forget their faces and they would all turn into feelings. They would all feel the same and they would all have the same face. I was sick of the reshapings of the same face. I was sick of eyes and ears and noses and mouths. They were all one—motherfuck they say daughterfuck—and they were all the same. They were all the Venuses in furs—gashes to gashes they say dicks to dicks—and all the penises too and they were the apple and the apple was the pair.

Aaron left and I followed him because it was going to be October soon and one of them joked something about the fruit of his loins and they all laughed and said it should go in the calendar—calendar they say calenture—and it made me feel sick as I left to go to the dining room as empty then as the front room was before. I poured myself more wine than before from one of the bottles and it spilled onto the table some and pooled around the mason jar.

Is my glass four-thirds full or is it one-third overflown, I asked Aaron.

He smiled and said, No worries.

It's all symbological. You stare at anything long enough and it ceases to exist. Your hand isn't yours anymore. But when you can't tell what's real and what isn't, does it really matter what it is. What if I were chewing on my hand and saying how it was the best apple I ever had.

So what're you doing now.

I'm just living on borrowed time. In that, I have a few months left before I have to start paying back the loans I took out. I still have quite a bit left, so I might just spend it all bacchanal.

He went into the kitchen then came back with some leftovers and some things they hadn't had for the calendar. He ate, but I wasn't hungry. He had brought out a glass bowl of blackberries and I reached for one and my mouth soured before I tasted it, but when I did it was good.

That's sour, I said.

Yeah.

But it's good.

His mouth was full, so he nodded.

I should really get going actually.

Okay man, nice meeting you.

Yeah same here. I drank another mouthful to finish the wine and I was slow to get up, but then some of the others came back into the dining room, so I started for the front room to say goodbye to Allison. She was wearing a flowery sundress, talking to the one with the calendar. I stood there until she saw me and she came over and up close to me until there wasn't more than a few inches between us and I could smell her breath and I knew mine was bad.

How are you.

Good, good.

Are you heading out.

Yeah.

Forever, she asked.

I laughed.

What've you been doing with yourself.

I don't know. I've been developing a rash, so that gives me something to do.

You look alright though, she said and she felt my jacket sleeve.

Yeah, the suit makes me want to itch it.

Scratch it.

Right. I always confuse itching with scratching.

I'm sorry we didn't get to talk as much.

Yeah, that's alright.

I went to the door and she opened it for me.

You seem good, I said.

I am.

Yeah.

Maybe see you soon if you're still around.

Yeah, sounds good. Goodbye.

It was cold and dark outside and I wouldn't know where I was going other than what direction I was headed. I walked in the middle of the street and could still sort of smell her breath. I had to stop when a light turned and I stood there and waited for it. When I left Allison in her bed I went to go home and burn all of my clothes in my bathtub because the fumigation wasn't enough and I knew it had all been for nothing. The light turned again and I remembered I should have told her how nice it was there.

When I came down to Telegraph Avenue I didn't want to head back, so I turned up the street then walked to the campus, which wasn't as far as I remembered it being from where I was. The white wine and weed had left my mouth dry, but I didn't stop to get something to drink, though I passed several bars along the way that I would pass by again when I headed back, so for the time being I felt like walking to clear my head.

I reached the southern edge of the campus and walked alongside it to the southeast end before I turned inside. Because it was winter the campus was empty because everyone went home. Saint Francis and I when we first started afternoon drinking would walk with beers in our bags through the southeast end where some of the bums laid around on their benches, though there was always one white-haired bum who stood around repeating himself to everyone and no one—Yeshua they say Noshua—whenever we passed by him to go drink. I walked past their benches, but I knew he wouldn't be there then.

The campanile counted the hours and I could hear it loud ringing again then a third time and I tried counting with it, but what was the measure of a man if most of his life was measured out in inches—give a man an inch they say and he'll take a knell—no, he would take a knee wouldn't he though, no, that was nihilism. I climbed over a chain fence while the hours rang a fourth and fifth then a sixth time before it was all quiet again, but where was the seventh I wondered as I walked through a field that went downhill. I must have miscounted, but what was the difference between six and seven at that time of evening, though as I was nearing the end of the field I could hear the buzz of sprinklers turning on and I started running for the end as some of them sprayed me— shut up they say shut up—and I got over the fence and onto the path again to catch my breath.

There were redwoods in a glade on the other side of a

wood bridge that crossed a stream and I stood on the bridge and listened for the water running, but the trees must have drank it all. I went to the other side and wandered through the redwoods and thought of the shit I used to think there. I thought of hearing someone else's voice in my head. I heard my own voice in my head. If I was talking to myself, I might as well speak up—do you see they say what I hear—since I was least alone when I was alone.

I turned left down the path to go toward the campanile and I looked up and could see it clearer when I came out from under the tall trees. The campanile was always lit when it was late enough. I had never been to the top and would never want to because it must have been the same as being at the bottom and looking up to see what time it was. Getting closer to the base though I couldn't see what time it was since the clock flattened against its side and the hands covered each other. I went around the base to where there were rows of plane trees I liked to go through in the winter because their leaves fell and all of their branches looked like roots and the trees looked like they were planted upside down to hold up the Earth.

When I got to the end I didn't feel like going farther, so I turned around and went through the trees again then turned right to go down the stairs where I could see the Golden Gate Bridge and some of the city. I reached into my breast pocket for the pack of cigarettes that was near full and I took one out to feel it between my thumb and finger while I found the white lighter in my other pocket to light the cigarette. I didn't smoke anymore, so I would have to finish the pack to make sure I didn't smoke anymore. I inhaled then let go of the smoke to pull it in through my nose, but still I couldn't, though it felt nice going straight to my head. I thumbed my lower lip then left the cigarette there. There was some light that wasn't coming from the city.

Should you be smoking if you sing, I asked Andrea.

Should I be smoking, she asked me.

I walked down the steps and started walking again and went downhill where there were other sorts of trees I had passed before with the poet laureate and I remembered him telling me all the names of the trees on the campus. He told me poets know the names of things. I didn't know the names of many trees. When I got closer to the west end of the campus I walked up to the Italian stone pines I liked to walk to because I knew their names and because one of them had a branch that bent down and ran along the ground until it curved up again to look like two trees. I went to sit down on the thick branch to finish the cigarette.

The day before last or maybe the day before, no, not the day before but New Year's Eve, Adam and I drank all of the afternoon walking in circles in downtown Los Angeles. There wasn't much else to do around the time of day most everyone else had half an hour or so to do nothing before they went where they were supposed to go. We didn't have anywhere we had to be until midnight and when we were done with what we had to drink and had nothing to do I thought we might just head home.

Adam turned to me and said, I had to fucking ask my mother for some money. We crossed and walked down the street and passed by some happy hours. I told her I'd pay her back by the end of the week but I only have the ten dollars of it left to pay her back with. Adam stopped outside of a market and I stood there while he felt some plums on the display, picking them up and thumbing their skin and pressing his fingers into their flesh before holding them up to the light and his nose but always putting them down again. I'm fuckin fucked man. He looked at me and I stared at the plum in his hand.

Yeah, I said. I don't know.

He went through several handfuls of plums then onto the next display as I walked around him and stood with my back to the one after that. There was a large piped structure set up on the sidewalk down the street a while that held up a number of paintings and there was a man in front of it with something of a crowd around him. They were laughing and he was loud.

What're we doing, I asked. I turned to Adam who had since moved from the small blue plums to the larger red ones and was feeling the difference between them while the older man with the paintings seemed to have the crowd sold on something else. We have to do something instead of all this shit.

What do you mean.

I don't know, I need do something with my days, like, start working or something.

Fuck man, I don't know about all that. Adam put a plum down to pick up another one then put that one down just as well to pick up another one. What do you wanna do, do you wanna fucking work, make a living like some of these fucks, no man, no fucking way, the only thing worse than being unemployed is being underemployed. He put a plum down. Look at you, you have all your days all to yourself.

I do nothing during most days but wait to drink at night.

Maybe you should start drinking during the day everyday. What do I know. It's much better to be doing nothing than to be doing anything and not be doing something. Adam picked up another pair of plums. I have no idea what I'm doing. You wanna do something, this is fuckin it man. He held the plums up in his palm and squeezed his fingers in and out of them. Why would I want to write when I can live, why would I paint when I can live, why act when I can live.

I don't know, you're a pretty good actor.

Everything isn't everything.

When I finished my cigarette I started walking again. I left the campus and walked over to the main street farther downtown where there were some bums and some other people walking and I felt good moving through them. The street smelled like a sewer and I walked under the lights that came from the streetlamps and ambered some of the closed storefronts. I came to an intersection and would have stepped out into the traffic if there were any right then. I lit another cigarette and kept walking.

There was some woman with a cigarette outside a market where there weren't any plums. She fidgeted in her high heels when I got close enough to not know how she wore a skirt like the one she did if she hadn't been holding a cigarette to her mouth while going through her purse without saying anything then looking up when she saw me and asking me for a light. I handed the lighter to her and I saw her hands were larger than mine and her fingers longer by about an inch or more while she lit her cigarette then looked at me again.

I'll suck your cock for twenty dollars, she said when she handed me back the lighter.

I don't have twenty dollars.

That's too bad.

How much would it cost me to suck yours.

Oh honey, I don't have a cock. She straightened out the front of her skirt as if I were supposed to not see something, but her voice was deep like she had started smoking as a little girl. I looked at her thick lips and her smooth and cream colored chin, though she didn't look very made up the way her skin looked lighter than it was in the dark. Her skirt came up around her thick tree trunk thighs almost to where a cock should have been somewhere in between them. What're you on.

I don't have twenty dollars, sorry but thank you, you're an absolute adon*ess*.

I turned to go and walked down another side street. It was getting cold and I clenched my teeth but I didn't feel as bad as before. I must have been walking forever but still counted my steps two to each slab of cement if there weren't any cracks in the concrete.

Step on a crack and break your mother's back, Adam said and I could still hear it in my head.

My foot was on the line and I walked into the street instead to stop looking down. There were no lines there. Andrea had said she hit her head on the concrete once didn't she. There must have been some sort of a scar on her forehead. Nostalgia was amnesia. Nostalgia was hitting my head on the concrete.

There was a Victorian house still on the same side street and I remembered it being there because it looked like a madhouse and I went onto the sidewalk to see it closer. The house always had the lights on whatever time it was. I stood there to light another cigarette and I dropped the other one at my feet to twist it into the ground between a crack and another line in the concrete.

Good evening.

It was an old woman I hadn't seen coming down the sidewalk until she passed me dressed like she was going to a funeral, though almost like she had just gotten out of the madhouse after such a long time that when she tried to act sane she could only manage to say good evening. She said it well enough, but they were always mumbling something to themselves, weren't they, though it was something they repeated like all the king's horses and all the king's men over and over again, but nobody said good evening to anybody anymore.

Good mourning, I said after her.

She didn't turn around, but again she must not have heard me over all the voices in her head—all the king's horses they say all the king's men—while she went along looking down at her steps, though she didn't turn to go into the madhouse because she might not have wanted me to see her recommit herself. I went over to the main street again and saw there were more and more people and maybe they were going out to drink or maybe they were going home to wake up tomorrow and go to church with their heads bowed down to kneel—all the king's whores and all the king's madmen—so I started up a side street on the other side.

Everything isn't everything, Adam repeated.

Isn't it.

Life and death, man. He shook his head. Life and death.

I stood there for a while then shrugged when Adam went inside to pretend to pay for the plums. I started over to stand in the crowd, though they were already leaving when I got to the paintings, the man walking with them down the street some, though he didn't seem to have sold anything to them or anyone else. The paintings were landscapes and I went to look closer at one and there was a label under it in a small cursive script that said to touch it. I reached out for it and there was a hand on my shoulder.

Don't touch that you fucker.

Adam laughed and I pushed his hand away and felt the edge of the canvas, which was thickly textured like sawdust almost like it was coming off. Adam stood there for a while before he tried touching the paintings too.

Hey who said you could touch those.

We both turned around and saw it was the man from before and he had a good hard laugh that Adam and I had to laugh too. The man had a full head of white hair and he was wrinkling around his eyes and mouth, but he didn't look too old. He held a brown bag in his hand he drank from. I smiled and looked at a few of the other paintings with the same label that said to touch them, but they all looked like they were of the same landscape.

These are really great, Adam said. I was gonna say they kinda remind me of being in Italy.

The man smiled as all the short white hairs around his mouth stretched across his brown skin with his lips held together and his eyes nearly closed until his blushed cheeks tightened then sank down toward his mouth and everything fell back into place again with them. Most of these were painted in Sicily.

Oh, my grandfather on my father's side is from Sicily. Adam stared at nothing while holding a finger to his mouth. I can't remember where exactly, I think it's something like, pasayco, peseco.

Ah Paceco yeah.

Paceco that sounds right, I think that might be it but I don't know. I wish I'd gone there though when I was over there. Adam scratched the back of his head. I was only there a semester though.

Well it's not too big an island, where in Sicily did you go.

I was actually only in Italy most of my time there. I never got to go to Sicily. I would've really liked to have gone, but I was mostly in Florence because I was working for a carpenter there for a while, but then I also went to Venice and Rome and that sort of thing, but yeah, Sicily.

It's a good place to be from and to go to too, and Paceco, Paceco is about as far to the west as you could go. The farther west you go in Sicily the better it is there, because everyone in the east is a tourist, well, maybe not everyone, there are also the ones living off all of the tourists, but the farther west you go is good, even if it's just the once to see where you're from. I was born outside of Agrigento, that's farther south and quite a bit east of Paceco, but then I mostly grew up in New York, but I still go there from time to time, between here and Sicily and New York, a few months here, a few months there, a few months there. He held the bag to his mouth and drank. When my brother gets here actually, we're driving home then going to New York and in two weeks Sicily.

Sounds like some trip, I said.

It's good to always be traveling. Everyone I know wherever I am keeps telling me I should be spending the entire year there instead of leaving to go somewhere else then always coming then going back and forth and back and forth but I like it, it keeps me young. You should go to Sicily too, it'll keep you from growing any older. He looked at his watch. What've you two been getting into today.

Nothing really.

Yeah, we've just been going around, not doing too much, just drinking all day really.

The man stared at a painting then looked to see if someone was walking down the sidewalk as he squinted at us. Hey, you guys want a beer. He swirled the brown bag in his hand.

I looked to Adam and we both shrugged and smiled, Sure. Yeah.

Adam and I followed the man around to the paneled van parked with one back door left open against the structure. He put the beer down on the bumper and swung the other one open and we could see there was nowhere else to leave the can because the back of the van was all large white buckets overflowing with art supplies, a number of canvases farther toward the front of the van and arranged against the wall, but just inside there was a cooler. He opened it to take a beer as he shook a bag open from a stack of small brown bags and slid the beer into it to set it down on the bumper and open the can before he handed it to Adam then did the same for me.

We held our beers together with several salutes, which turned into introductions and we stood around drinking. The beer was cold and sweated through the brown of the bag and we drank until Adam became Adamo in Giovanni's mouth and the more Giovanni drank, the more everything he said sounded Sicilian, though it was the same for Adam.

What I wanted to ask you actually cause I notice you keep saying Sicilia then Italia and then Sicilia again was, do the different regions take precedence over Italia or does everyone prefer to be called Italiano.

I think most Italians do, but Sicilians don't, but then again I'm Siciliano, but you know sometimes it's a very big difference. My mother was born in northern Italy, she wasn't

198

Sicilian like my father was, she was born a bit outside of Rimini.

Rimini. Adam made a face like he had heard it before. Where is that again.

It's in the north, in Emilia-Romagna, Rimini, maybe some twenty miles south of Ravenna.

Okay yeah.

But if she was born another few hundred meters south from where she was born she would've been a Sammarinese, she would have been born in San Marino, which you know is its own thing, its own region, separate from everything else in Italy, no taxes no army no nothing, everything is good, that's if she were Sammarinese though, but there's big differences either way you look at it in south and north and west and east, just like in Sicilia.

Right.

We drank and I listened to them go on and I drank.

Salvatore, Giovanni said looking down the sidewalk where there was a man coming up to the van and he was somewhat rounded in his face and body and was black-haired and well-trimmed all around. He came up to Giovanni. This is my brother, Salvatore. We all shook hands and Adam was Adamo again while Giovanni went into the cooler and readied a beer in a bag for Salvatore. This is Adamo, his father is from Paceco.

My grandfather actually, my father was actually also born in New York.

Yeah okay, grandfather.

When Giovanni offered his brother the beer, Salvatore said something in Italian and Giovanni said something else and handed it to me instead. We need to get packing soon, Giovanni said and shrugged as Salvatore went around to start with the canvases while Giovanni gathered all the finished beers into one of the buckets. You reap what you sow is what our father used to say, though you know how it is, Salvatore was born in New York fifty two years ago, and never been to Italia until we're going next week, which is because he was born here, we're eleven years apart, but we were supposed to have two sisters between the two of us.

They don't want to hear about our dead siblings, Salvatore said.

Giovanni shrugged again. It's good to be around family still. Do you have any siblings.

I have an older sister and brother, Adam said. They're much older than me though.

You're both younger, and young, that's good. Giovanni threw his beer in the bucket. You guys done, you want another beer. He was already opening the cooler to give us another beer before I had finished the one he had just handed to me. Okay I think that's it, I'll get to packing.

Do you need any help with anything, I asked.

Yeah did you want us to do anything, Adam said.

No, that's alright, I know where everything goes so it's faster if we take it down ourselves. He patted me on both shoulders since I was holding a beer in each hand. Thank you though.

Thank you.

Yeah, thanks.

Adam and I stood there and drank and didn't know what to say to each other but we smiled as we moved back to give them room and wait on the sidewalk, though they had only started to take down the paintings and lean them for the time being against the structure. Adam tiptoed back and forth on the curb where there was some water in the gutter while I finished one of the beers and I went back to the van and put it in the bucket with the others. They started to rearrange everything on the sidewalk and I went back over to Adam as they started to move the canvases into the van. Adam and I drank and walked the few steps from the curb into the street with nothing else to do and I started to feel all the drinking from the afternoon.

I feel like Giovanni has become this mythical father figure, Adam said. We were just taken in by him and sheltered from the storm then nurtured back to health and now we're brothers, like he is the father that took us out of the wild, that's what it is, man, he's our father and we're Romulus and Remus, but now our father is sending us off into the wilderness again.

Yeah.

Rome never fell. We are Rome.

I could only laugh at Adam while he went on until they came over again and everything taken out of the van had been put back where it was and all the pipes and paintings gone and we shook hands again and it was mostly ciaos and an arrivederci before they were gone too. We stood there and watched them leave before we turned to go down the street the way we came and we walked through a park until we got to a fountain. Adam stopped and looked at where we were going and how the sun had come down since we had left the van. We sat down and finished our beers at the fountain and left them there and started to the metro.

I miss our father, he said.

Me too, brother, me too.

I miss my father.

I came around another corner and could almost hear the campanile ringing again but I couldn't well enough to count the time with it. There was a blonde I tried not to look at and I stared at my steps while she walked toward me.

Hey sorry, do you know where Telegraph Avenue is. Her voice was thick and her hair brushed back behind her ears, her eyes green and her bottom lip pierced.

Yeah. I looked the other way and felt turned around, so I looked back and it was the way I was already headed. It's just down the street here a while, it's up ahead like a minute.

Ah alright, thanks.

I started walking and could see her walking next to me and I slowed down a bit, but then she turned to me. I usually don't take the train out here, so I'm just a little lost, sorry.

You're okay. It's just up ahead.

I have to meet up with my friend, we're driving to New Mexico tomorrow.

Oh, New New Spain. I held the cigarette to my mouth. What takes you to the promised land.

My friend takes me, she said. She only had the bag in her hand and the bag on her back.

Nice. My friend and I might also be going to the promised land.

What's the promised land.

Where the tree of life is.

We were almost there when she turned to me again and said, You don't look too good.

Yeah. I laughed. Long night.

It's not even seven is it.

Yeah, I'm just sort of lighting the cigarette at both ends right now.

Why would you light a cigarette at both ends.

I'm all out of candles.

We walked a while then she asked, Are you good.

Good, I asked. I don't know, I don't think I'm that bad.

No, I mean, do you have any weed.

Oh, no. Sorry. I'm all out of everything.

She laughed and I was about to turn to go walk another side street when she said, Hey could I actually have one of those.

Yeah, here. I gave her a cigarette and saw how small and soft her hand looked when I lit it for her. Right, well, safe travels.

Thanks so much.

I walked down the side street and I felt good to do something good for someone. I finished the cigarette and plucked one of my hairs and it was thin and I could barely see it in the lamplight. It was always the last time with Amy and it was always at her place with all the white sheets and all the white.

I wondered what was the worst thing I had ever done—first the worst they say second base—maybe it was when my cousin kissed me and I wanted to touch her, but she wouldn't let me, so I went and told on her that she kissed me.

After Adam had dropped me off yesterday, after the diner and before we went to the co-op, I went to go see Amy. That was bad too. I told her how Adam and I were going on a road trip up north and she said, Nobody goes on a north-south road trip.

Why not.

Everyone goes west-east.

We might go east.

Why don't you call me mon Amy anymore, she asked me.

Do you want me to call you something if you tell me to call you it.

It sounds the same to me.

I don't know.

Are you okay.

Yeah, I'm just unhappy.

I can make you happy for a little while but then you have to go.

Her hand was a tree around my cock with her palm up and down until I was hard in her mouth and I went to put my hand in between her legs, but she didn't want to. She never did.

Are you laughing at me or crying, I asked her after she came back from the bathroom.

Laughing. Both. I don't know. Laughing at us.

Are you crying for us too.

No I don't think we deserve it.

We always want what we don't want.

Why do you only let me into your head and not your heart.

My head is where my heart is.

Come on.

Come on what, I've made myself so sad over you.

Me too.

Me too means nothing to me. You didn't have to.

I'm so lonely.

You're so lovely.

I don't like love.

I like how you look.

Yeah, yeah.

Isn't that enough to say that.

You're not a good person, but you're a better friend.

One of us has to be the better friend so one of us can be the better friend. One of us has to be a worse one. Adam and I, the only reason we are friends is we were friends.

You're so bad.

I'm only as bad as he is.

Adam knows I went down on you, did you know that.

No, I didn't. You didn't have to tell him that.

He thought it wasn't his.

I guess you can't give birth from giving head. Well, what are you gonna do.

I don't know.

You know, I thought of all the things I might have said that would have made things different. Maybe us ending up together, maybe I could've made us both happy.

What might you have said.

It doesn't matter. None of my lines worked.

Your lines, she laughed. Things would be a lot easier for you if you didn't try so hard.

Yeah, but I like you.

You don't like me as much as you like seeing yourself in me.

That sounds like something I would say.

I walked for a while until I heard a voice that was loud in the empty street that it sounded like it came from everywhere, sung between shallow breaths with drawn-out vowels, I stood still and listened to try to tell where it was coming from, but it ended and I could tell there was nothing to see there.

What are you that I can't see you, are you some god.

No one said nothing.

Some god you are, I can see you for what you are.

It wasn't too bad a walk back, but my head spun all the way there and I wondered what else I couldn't see. All the things I couldn't see if I hadn't seen them—all the king's horses they say all the king's men—like all the conquistadors and all their ships off the coast and like all the king's horsemen and like the Chimera.

Chimera.

Come era.

Chi me Ra.

Chime Ra.

Cum era.

Come.

Saint Francis and I stood at the back behind everyone else in their gray folding chairs with brown leather seats set up wall to wall in several rows in the long, thin room with walls covered in black and white and brown and red with paintings that looked like staring into someone else's head. We stood at the back of the reading but closer to the front of the gallery, next to a table with boxes of wine, drinking out of plastic wine glasses. They were almost out of white.

I never drink a drink out of the glass it's supposed to be drunk out of, I said.

I'm drunk, Saint Francis said and he raised his glass and swirled the little wine left in it.

They're always running out of white wine before red. Why don't people just have more white.

Because we drink it all.

White wine is the drink of the people.

Why don't you just drink the red.

I'm allergic to red.

I've seen you drink red.

Yeah but it gets me drunk like a fuck, like I'm allergic to it or something.

Everyone is allergic to alcohol.

Maybe, but no, I can't drink too much. Red wine always hits me like whiskey because I think I'm allergic to the sulfites or the tannins or whatever else is in it, though whiskey I can drink like water, so you know. It is what it isn't.

Feels syllogistic.

The whole room applauded something, so I slapped my palm against my leg. I tried the white wine box again and pushed the tab down then held up the box and tried to shake it into the glass, but there was nothing, so I filled my glass with red instead. Saint Francis poured himself another glass while I swirled the red wine in mine to see the branches of red stick to the sides until they ran back to the bottom.

Adam got out of his seat at the back of the rows of chairs

and pushed it screeching against the concrete floor of the gallery far enough to get out of the row. He had changed out of his suit and was now wearing a yellow paisley shirt he said was a woman's blouse because the buttons were buttoned the opposite way. The pattern was part of the pattern. He pushed his seat forward back into the row then came over and whispered to me, This fuck says he can get us some amanitas.

Okay.

So I need some cashish.

Fuck you. No. I'm cutting you off.

Come on man, Adam raised his voice and someone looked back at us so he whispered again. We'll split it halfway.

It's for your own good.

What happened, Saint Francis asked.

Well I didn't really want to pay for it, I mostly wanted to find them myself and to not have to pay for them, but I can get us some amanitas if you guys want to split it with me.

I'm in, Saint Francis said.

He's in, Adam turned to me and so did Saint Francis.

Fuck you fucks, I'm tired. I'm just gonna drink some red wine and have a bad time. You guys can do whatever you want.

Mother of fuck, nada. Don't fucking throw up.

I'll throw up if I want to. Vomiting has gotten me out of a lot of things I didn't want to be in.

Yeah right.

Let's just leave. They're out of white wine and there's no one I wanna fuck here.

No I'm gonna try to talk him down on the amanitas.

How much does he want for how much.

I don't know.

Probably too much.

Is anything else happening tonight.

There always is, isn't there.

I think someone mentioned something last night, Saint

Francis said.

Are we gonna go to that, Adam asked him.

I don't know.

How was your thing, Adam asked me.

It was good. A lot of naked women. The most naked women I've ever seen right there in front of me. They were still trying to cover themselves up with all these vegetables and what not. You would've loved it too. They had all this fucking fruit there, ripe, homegrown, good for you.

Ah did you grab anything.

No I was in an altered state of mind.

Man.

Just have some red wine and feel fine.

Fuck wine, Adam said and he went back to his seat at the back and pulled it out then in to the row as it made a sound along the floor of the gallery again and he waved an apology to someone.

The tall brunette left the stage, which was nothing more than several steps that led to the other half of the gallery. She thanked everyone and I turned to Saint Francis and said, She's very pretty her. Very pretty for a tall woman.

She is, isn't she.

She is something else.

Her and Anna live together now.

She has a really good posture for how tall she is.

Anna went up to the stage and wrestled with the microphone stand to shorten it but then gave up and moved it down one step and leaned closer to talk into it. Everyone laughed as she smiled at them then looked at her notes.

Thank you, she said and she applauded and everyone applauded again. And thank you all for coming too. We're really hoping to make this a regular thing. So I'm so glad you're all here for it. But without further ado up next we have Alain.

Anna applauded again then left the stage as a tall man in a

yellow fisherman jacket walked up the steps and moved the microphone stand up and everyone laughed again. The unshaven top of his head had his hair stand up in a puff of curly brown. He didn't say anything but instead stood there with his hands in his jacket pockets like he was trying to look at nothing until he stared up into the audience.

This guy's good, Saint Francis said. He reminds me of you.

Fuck off.

Saint Francis laughed while I tried not to listen and I drank a mouthful of the red wine, which tasted like vinegar and made my mouth itch and my tongue swell. I swirled the wine in the glass and stared at the veins on the side again.

Fuckin blood alcohol, I said.

Saint Francis shrugged.

I am a minotaur, the poet said with a French accent. Half the shit I say is bullshit.

Everyone laughed.

My head is horny, he said as he made horns out of his hands and put them on his head.

Most everyone nodded as his cadence left them waiting for him to go on.

If we're all ears how do we see. Do you see what I mean.

I turned to Saint Francis and tried to talk, but it was hard with my tongue swollen in my mouth when I tried, so I repeated myself. Now I am become deaf, destroyer of words.

The poet waited like he was done, so I drank and had a harder time swallowing the wine.

Down with the bourgeoisie. Up with proletariat.

Someone cheered and the poet pointed at them and smiled.

Lower with the upper middle class, upper with the lower middle class.

I said to Saint Francis, It's easier to be ironic when you have nothing to be sincere about.

I don't think this has anything to do with irony.

It's easier to stand against something than to stand for it.

Well, of course it is.

It's hard to do things.

Yeah.

It's hard to get drunk twice in one day.

Usually you do the one drunk the whole day.

I just want to get back to pre-post-modernism.

Was that ever a thing.

Post-post-modern is just modern, pre-modern maybe.

Yeah.

If it's been said before, don't say it, unless that's what you're trying to say.

I'm feeling pretty drunk.

We're so postmodern now we can't even see modern anymore. Modern was good, modern told the truth. Postmodern just retells the telling. You have to go through postmodern to get to modern now. You can't not address postmodern, but the word postmodern still has the word modern in it.

The poet had quieted down and I looked up again as he said, Rhyme is criminal.

Everyone else applauded.

I laughed and said, Poets always have to have pauses in between their poems when they read them so the audience knows when to applaud.

One, the poet said then he said something in French. Two, he continued then again something in French. Three. Something in French. Four. French.

It was almost all in French and the higher he counted the longer the French, but everyone was into it and I drank in mouthfuls to finish my glass and pour myself another one.

Eight.

Adam looked back a few times and I made a motion for us to leave, but he shook his head.

Eleven.

A small sort of terrier dog with a cone around its neck came up to me with its tail wagging. He was shaved in some places and when I bent down to look closer at him I saw that he was covered in stitches. I scratched him where he wasn't.

Fourteen.

He looked like he was on something and it must have felt good to him being on what he might have been on and staring up at me I wondered if it would do the same for me what it did for him.

Fifteen.

The cone was as large on his body as his body was small.

Sixteen.

The cone was painted on with thick splotches on the outside like a sculpture in the round with bright but chipping colors, standing out from the white-and-black inside where there were three words written in different handwriting I couldn't read, though I didn't think the dog could either.

Everyone applauded and Anna came up to the stage again and this time stood on her tiptoes to talk into the microphone and say, We're gonna take a break. Please help yourself to some wine.

Well I think we got here at just the right time, I said. Let's leave before it ends.

I wanna hang around some.

Why.

Anna put all of this together.

We moved away from the table as some of the others came to fill their glasses up from the red wine boxes. Their teeth and tongues were red when they opened their mouths.

It's a good turn out, I said.

Yeah.

She won't miss us.

Yeah she will.

Adam came over to us again and said, Almost got the amanitas.

Good.

Well alright, should we stay. The breaks are the best part, but let's leave when the break's over.

Maybe, Saint Francis said and we followed him through the rows of chairs to a circle that had formed closer to the stage.

Anna looked at all of us like she didn't know what to say and she said nothing. She smiled and looked down at her notes. They were all there as far as I could tell but there must have been more of them coming, the way they talked. Saint Francis went to stand next to Anna while Adam and I fell between the tall brunette and a shorter one wearing a yellow fisherman jacket the same as the French poet. Adam introduced himself while I drank and listened to some of the others.

Anna, Adam asked the one in the fisherman jacket. Isn't she Anna. He pointed at Anna.

Yeah but she goes by Anna Lee when there's the two of us.

And you just go by Anna.

Well we live together, so she's always Anna Lee.

Interesting.

Though I've been spending more time on Alain's boat. He lives on a boat in the bay.

Anna had nice hair and a nice enough face, but her body was lost in the yellow, though maybe seeing me she wondered what she would look like in a suit. She was beautiful but looked like she tried not to be, which was always attractive, the amount of effort it must have took, her hair short and brown like she had cut it herself and had cut his hair too, but their hair didn't stand the same, their complexion different despite her effort. She was sunburned and sniffling, maybe because of the sea or maybe because she was allergic to the red wine or the dog, but still she must have been something to look at before she tried hard to not look like she did.

So what's with the dog, Adam asked everyone.

Cain didn't come with a collar, Anna Lee said.

Yeah there wasn't a number to call for Rex, Anna said.

Cain Rex, I asked.

They acted like they had said a few times over the same story of how the three of them, Anna Lee and her roommates, had found him half dead on the side of the road, though when they took him in to see what they could do and seeing there was no one else there the three of them agreed they would take him home themselves. Everyone laughed at how they still couldn't agree on one name between the three of them.

They said each name they had given him and that with each name he was different.

Laika was the tall brunette's name for him because the cone resembled a space helmet to her, so one third of it was painted with Laika in space surrounded by several constellations.

Anna gave him the name Rex because the cone resembled a crown and she painted a third of it in branches like a crown of thorns, though instead of having thorns themselves there were teeth like tyrannosaur teeth, smooth and white in the absence of paint, the cone itself being drawn out of a thick brown around them. The teeth were sunk in the impasto as if biting into the plastic, the branches brown and the teeth white because of them.

There was Cain too, short for Canine. Anna Lee had written in thick black impasto on a third of the cone what looked like poetry, numbered verses and a paw print near the end. Cain was a good name.

A good name is a man's best friend, I said.

Or a woman's, Anna said.

Huh.

Why does it have to be a man.

It's just how the saying goes.

That's not even a saying, a good name is a man's best

friend.

I think I heard it somewhere, Saint Francis said.

Of course you did.

We have this tendency to name things after ourselves, to name ourselves after things, and we want them to be good, like Cain.

Well, thanks. Anna Lee smiled at me.

The tall brunette turned to me and said, Anna Lee says you're such a great poet.

That's nice of her. Usually my reputation recedes me.

Well, she's said other things too.

They're all true, I smiled at the tall brunette.

These paintings are great, Adam said. Who did them.

It's an artist in San Francisco, Anna said. He's very raw.

I can see that.

Adam and Anna and the tall brunette went to look at one of them and Saint Francis and Anna Lee closed the circle in on me.

What're you reading tonight, she asked me.

I'm not reading.

Don't you know how.

No I just don't have anything to read.

Come on, Saint Francis said. You should read something.

I can't.

Can't or won't.

I won't because I can't.

You won't because you can't or you can't because you won't.

Anna frowned and her hair was short red and almost curlicue, her freckles almost as bright on her face and her neck and arms, fitting her well enough like her pale skin. Saint Francis looked at her and I could tell how well something was going on between them. When we first got there and she came to the back, she hugged Saint Francis much longer than Adam or me, though she hadn't seen me in over a year and she had never seen Adam before.

I don't know, I said. Pick one.

Oh, okay. Doesn't know how to read, Anna said while she read from the paper.

The two of them looked down at her notes and the less than half a page left for the rest of the night. Anna had a sleeveless black crayon that she rolled up and down the page and made a few dark shaded streaks on everything written in pen from before.

Well, I said. I'm gonna go get another glass of wine.

Okay, I'll just write you down for going at the end, and we'll see how you feel then.

Yeah we'll see how I feel then, I said and went to get another glass of wine then came back to where Adam was standing alone in front of one of the paintings that looked like a Rorschach test.

What is that, I asked.

It says it's human matter.

Like what.

This one is menstrual blood and semen.

What's it called.

It's untitled.

Should call it fetus.

Yeah.

What do you see.

Sunny side up or over easy.

I looked at the other paintings then back to the one we were looking at and said to Adam, This is so vulgar all these paintings of vaginas.

Some of them are penises I think.

Untitled is the worst thing that ever happened to art.

Adam didn't have anything to say.

Maybe self-portraits are actually.

Untitled self-portraits.

Motherfuck.

We walked over to the next painting and I forced down a mouthful of wine.

What do you think it means.

I'm thinking about these colors though, he said.

Brown is browner than beige is beige.

That's true.

Red is redder than pink is pink.

That's the same thing.

White is blacker than red is red.

It's not about white and black.

It's white and red, right.

No, it's the colors themselves.

I had to have looked the most out of place, standing out in black and white against the sort of counterculture that didn't go much farther than colorful close-cut hair and clothes.

I offered Adam the glass of wine and told him, It's just grapes man.

Yeah but it's not raw.

It's good for you.

We should get out of here.

These paintings are such shit.

They are shit.

I agree, I said and finished the wine.

Me too.

I'd rather doubt my greatness than deny my shittiness.

This guy's shittiness is his greatness.

I like that tall brunette.

Why're you talking to me then.

What's her name.

She didn't say.

I feel like I'm already heartbroken over her.

Why're you telling me that.

It feels good to feel bad. It feels good to just feel. Just feel it. Bad is good. It feels good all the bad I feel now will someday feel good. Maybe I'll read something and she'll fall in love with me.

Do it.

She'll probably want me to read some of her poetry too. Which'll of course only make me fall out of love with her. I looked over at the tall brunette and how it didn't matter how tall she was if she were on her knees to suck out the poison—poison they say poisson—but her hands would be bigger than mine, but still I didn't want to read her shit. All I want is to be quoted.

Then go fuckin talk to her, nada. I wanted to leave when you got here, but we can stay here if you really wanna stay. There are a lot of women here to fuck.

I don't know. Let's just go. I don't want to fuck any women I haven't already fucked.

Fuck that.

Fucked that.

I went to get another glass of wine and sat down in one of the seats toward the back where the dog walked over to me again with his mouth open and his tongue out, so I picked him up and sat him in my lap. He stayed there for a while but then started wrestling with me. I helped him down onto the ground where he walked circles around in his small body made for foxhunting before he was picked up by the tall brunette and walked around a while then put down again to play like he was dead. The tall brunette scratched him where the cone started at his scruff and he rolled over to have her scratch him more before he ran off and went barking toward the door as the doorbell rang after him. Someone went to get the door and the dog came back after some of them, barking as loud as they all were again.

Anna Lee went up to the stage again and I went back toward the table where Adam stood with some of them who had just gotten there and were loud pouring themselves some wine. Anna Lee said nothing and stood behind the mic-

217

rophone until Saint Francis shouted for them to shut up and when they did she didn't have to say anything else for them to sit down.

She mouthed a thank you to Saint Francis and he nodded then came back to the table.

Anna Lee reread her notes and looked up and down at everyone there, covering her mouth and making a sort of smothered *ch ch chem* sound, laughing to herself until it sounded fake with how quiet it was as we all looked at her. She stopped rolling the crayon against the paper. She smiled then closed her mouth only to run her tongue over her teeth and smile again. She looked up and down at her notes and they were mostly quiet who weren't drinking.

Well let's get back on track. I think Anna also had something to say, she said and left the stage to go sit down in the front row.

Some of the ones who had just gotten there were still pouring their glasses of red wine and the ones who had been there from earlier helped ourselves to more.

I think it's done, Saint Francis said while he shook one of the boxes into a glass.

Good.

Adam looked to me to leave and I looked to Saint Francis but he held up an index finger as he filled up a glass of red wine from another box to pass it to me and I tried to pass to Adam, but he held up his hand and I shrugged at Saint Francis and kept the second glass for myself to drink.

One of the others came over to me and asked, Hey man did I miss Alain.

Who.

The poet in the yellow jacket.

Oh, yeah. You did.

Damn.

Just missed him.

Fuck.

It was really great though. He's a really fuckin great poet.

He stared at me for some reason, so I drank until he walked away.

Anna came up to the microphone then stepped to the side and asked, Can you all hear me.

Most of them said they did and she sat down on the top step.

Okay, so I should preface this by saying where I got the inspiration for this. She flattened her hair against her head. What I actually wanted to talk about is what I've been working on, what I don't really know what to call, other than what I've been calling it at the time being. Dare.

Someone laughed and I finished another glass.

Anna spoke with a clockwise turning of her hands that she repeated in front of her chest, but it didn't sound like she wasn't as happy to be there. She went on, Dare stands for dead animal resurrection exhibit. Or, dead animal resurrection experiment, I'm not sure which one yet. But it pretty much is what it sounds like, sort of this found art project which I first got the idea from Rex. We first saw him when he was just laying there on the side of the road and I could feel his little heart beating, which was like this experience of death, in what I guess you'd call a primal or primordial way. She scratched the top of her head before going back to the clockwise turning of her hands. I think maybe I'm not really explaining it right, like, last week, when I was walking on the beach, I came across this beached whale, which must have died not too long ago and was just laying there in the sand, before anyone had gotten to him, so what I did was I just stripped down right there.

The French poet came to the back and stood next to me, so I motioned at Saint Francis to pour me another one. I didn't feel like staying much longer, but Adam didn't seem to want to leave and Saint Francis seemed the same. The poet had sunned and salted skin, leathery and tan, which was worn like the only time he ever washed was a swim in the sea, though it must have made his hair stick up in small curls like it did.

The dog came back over to some of the people that had just gotten there like he knew them.

So, I'm lying down next to it, face down in the sand, like it was. And I was feeling it, feeling it and the vibrations of it in me, feeling the whale passing through me, almost like it was on its way out but was still sort of there in the time while it went through me.

I drank and looked at Cain. I didn't know what death was, but I knew it was something bigger than a beached whale.

I think the whole thing is that it resurrects in you and you really get to know death, that's then the whole idea of dare, I think it would be something to really consider for our art space. To have these ceremonial exhibits for people to come closer to death and see how it relates to them and to see how so much of it comes through the musicality of dare, in the vibrations that you really feel as it relates to art, the resurrection of the dead animal exhibited as art. So, yeah. That's it.

They were all quiet except for Cain, but then they weren't.

I always wanted to slaughter a chicken.

A sacrifice to our gods.

A sacrifice to our stomachs.

They laughed.

I don't think this is something to not be serious about.

Everyone faces death a certain way.

That's true.

I actually have a poem about this.

Why does everything you write have to be so apocalyptic.

I don't know, why does the world have to end.

I've always wanted to slaughter an animal to know the whole process of eating an animal.

That's awful.

What do you mean.

Slaughtering a chicken, I don't think we'll be doing that, right Anna Lee.

I don't know.

Maybe not a chicken then, how about a rabbit.

Yeah maybe a rabbit.

That's even worse, Anna said and she stood up.

Rabbit stew.

How is that worse.

We should probably leave soon, I said to Saint Francis.

Yeah alright, he said and finished his glass.

Adam came over to me smiling and I finished my glass too.

Something small to understand what sort of life you're taking.

What're you talking about.

For breakfast or lunch, or brunch.

Maybe we could even get the rabbit fur and skin and make a pelt.

We'd have to learn how to do that.

I don't understand how you could do that.

Well we'll learn how to.

It's a very native sort of thing to do though isn't it, using all of the animal.

We could even plug instruments into the bodies to use them as amplifiers.

We could do the slaughter and then do the whole dead animal thing as well.

No, we can't. Those are two different things. What you're doing. What you're all saying is just taking an animal's life while what I'm saying is celebrating its death through a resurrection.

Anna looked to Anna Lee to say something, but she didn't. They were talking about the sort of things they didn't know much about. They were talking about things like life and death, good and bad, things paired together because of how different they thought they were as things set apart by how close they really were, but neither Anna knew what to say.

I drank until there was nothing left to drink, no, there was nothing to drink and there was nothing to snort and there was nothing left for us to do, but everyone moved in one motion and there was no telling where the others might be. I pressed up against her, the same one from before, faceless under the brim of her white cowboy hat, her hair curling down under it and thick with sweat, her ass soft against me. She pushed against me harder back and forth to try to feel something against her ass, but there was nothing.

We were dancing on a picnic table and holding onto the pipes running across the ceiling same as all the others did on their own tables or in the spaces on the floor in between tables. There was someone against my back and I turned around and saw the other blonde I was dancing with and I held onto her as she took the black cowboy hat from my head and became faceless again, turning around, her ass soft and my cock hard again.

Adam danced by himself in a circle that had opened up for him after he had too much to drink but still not enough. I tried to get the two of them to come down the table with me and get one of them up against him, but it was too much to do so we danced without trying to move. The blonde behind me handed me a beer that was half empty while the song sounded like it would never end and I turned around.

They danced against me and I drank while they twisted and tightened against me, the same as before, feeling the sound, which was good, the sound coming and going. It was always the same sound over and over again, but there was no difference in time, the sound had no time to tell, the sound only ever on or off or on again.

I turned around and felt her ass against me and pulled her in closer and I looked down into the crowd and saw Adam stood there purpling where he was. He must have seen all the lost ones and how none of them were much more than repetitions of each other or repetitions of me. The place wasn't dead but dying. I threw the bottle into the crowd and hoped it turned someone's head red and didn't wait for the sound to turn over and start up again.

I could use some fresh air and a cigarette, I said to the one in the black cowboy hat.

I pushed her away and someone replaced me when I got down from the table and as I walked through them all I felt how slow they were where they stood. I walked until I was outside where there was smoke and there were all the firebreathers.

I took a cigarette out and there was a second hand asking me for one, so I put a cigarette in its palm as well. I lit mine and looked up and saw how she looked like Audra. I lit her cigarette and asked her how she got there.

I live here.

Right.

Why do you ask.

Don't I know you.

I don't think so.

Do you know Adam.

Yeah.

I know Adam too.

Yeah I know Adam.

I think I'm suffering from the delirium tremendous.

What're you on.

Nothing that good.

Oh okay. Do you know if my ex is here. Her name is Molly.

Are you into girls, well, she's your ex, so you must be or must have been, but aren't now.

She leaned in to my ear and said, The drug.

I don't think anyone here minds if you're doing drugs. You don't have to whisper.

I'm whispering so they don't ask for some as well. And I'm not whispering, you're yelling.

Okay, I whispered. I think I can get you some. Let me finish this cigarette.

Yeah let's do Molly.

You and me.

Yeah you and me.

I know I know you from somewhere.

Where.

I think I've been here before. Isn't your name Annie.

Allie. Annie is my sister's name.

I don't know any Annies. What is Allie short for.

Alexandra.

Your parents named you and your sister Alexandra and Anexandra, that's odd.

No they didn't.

Is she your twin.

No but we look a lot alike.

That's good. She's very pretty.

Aren't you something, what's your name.

They call me Dionysus. I am ecstasy.

Are we gonna do ecstasy then.

The drugs and the drinking has been done to death. We're not dead are we.

No. Are you okay.

Yeah I'm alive for the time being. I'm trying to give up the pills and all their certainty, but you know, another one more couldn't hurt. My head, you know, isn't screwed in all the way. Let's just finish our cigarettes and do another round.

That sounds good.

You and me, Annie.

Allie.

Audra.

Allie.

Audra Allie Annie, what's the difference. I like you. You remind me of someone I know. Do you know you look just like Audra.

Who's Audra.

Someone who looks just like Andrea.

I don't know any Andreas.

I don't either.

Who is she.

Someone who looks just like you.

Who are you.

They call me the sun god Ra. I know it sounds somewhat heliocentric, but I'm a golden god.

What.

We spend the night drinking remembering what we can remember from other nights we spent drinking the night remembering drinking. You forget about someone by finding someone else.

Where are you from.

What.

Where do you live.

I'm sort of in between places right now.

Oh yeah, moving is the worst.

I'm the worst.

It's not that bad.

We were crowded on the small balcony and most of them were trying to inhale as much of the secondhand smoke as they could. I looked down at my cigarette and wondered whether I would burn through one of the wings printed near the filter or both.

I regret everything I've ever done simply because it was done. If I've done anything I've ruined everything. Life is death. Life is a succession of failures followed by defeat. Yeah, I don't want to do this anymore. I don't wanna drink, but then again I do. I don't need alcohol as much as alcohol needs me. It always will. In heaven I'd be an ambrosiac and in hell, well, I'd still be an alcoholic. I like to drink. It keeps the voices in here quiet and makes the voices out there bearable. Drown out the voices before they sink you. So what difference is it if the world is good and my head isn't or if my head is and the world isn't, there's still that difference. My head isn't like other heads.

Oh.

You're good, dear. I like you.

I like you too.

The good ones are the ones that are good when you're bad.

You're not so bad yourself.

Listen, I gotta get outta here. Do you know where's Adam. Inside maybe.

Yes the way in is the way out. Well, if you'll excuse me I'm gonna go self-destruct.

Are we gonna go do Molly.

Yeah, yeah, I'll find her. You stay here where I can see you.

I left the one who looked like Audra but could still hear all the firebreathers and their forked tongues whispering with the sharpness of their *s*'s there was always something to drink, but I did want to not drink. Inside I moved through them as they danced in the way again, passing some of the leftover tables pushed to the sides of the room to open it up for more dancing. I got to the end of the room and looked through the empty bottles and cans and saw they had poured almost all of their drinks into one large cooler. I turned the red syrup over and stirred it into a cup and drank. It was sugary and didn't taste like it was bad but like there was nothing in it. I finished the cup then started on another one and I drank until I felt sick—sick they say sic—and I waited to do another. I would find Adam and tell him the one who looked like Audra was looking for him. They were all on something or other that would last them the rest of the night, but sleep was the drug, soma—soma soma they say so so mama—and all that was left for me was for the night to end. I drank and wondered how long the drinking would take until I woke up home.

When I came to all I wanted was to roll over and go back to bed, so I turned but then fell onto the carpet and it smelled wet. I opened my eyes and I could see the woman all in black with the head of a panther staring at me with her round yellow eyes that I could barely make out the rest of her in the corner of the room. I closed my eyes and the sunlight was a warm red on them and when I opened them again she wasn't there and it felt good to wake up somewhere else.

I sat up and saw my jacket rolled up into a pillow on the couch. My shirt was unbuttoned and one of my nipples was hard and hurt, but the other one wasn't. I rubbed the other one until it also became hard, but it still didn't hurt. I stood up and scratched then stretched myself.

The morning was bright coming through the front door, but when I went to close it I saw Saint Francis on the porch couch and a black cat asleep on his stomach, so I left the door open for both of them. I went back and looked out the bay window and I saw the car was still there on the other side of the street. The last time I had been to see Eve was the same time I was here a year and not too long ago, early in the morning like it was again.

Adam was breathing heavily with his face in the couch, curled up into himself like a child, his jacket around most of himself. I went over and shook him and he moaned then he rolled over and I saw his face for the first time again, no longer childlike, the swelling had died down like he was some years older than the rounded face of several days ago. I pulled his jacket up over him again, staring at him, there was only the sound of his breathing through his mouth, breathing heavy like a manchild, his smile still somewhere under his breath.

I went over to the sink and drank water from the faucet in cupped handfuls and it ran down to my elbows and to my rolled up sleeves. I could smell how bad I smelled and how bad my breath was, so I walked down the hall to take a shower before everyone else used up the hot water. I had some time since the hall was still dark, but I could hear someone upstairs, maybe just the pipes or maybe someone using the upstairs shower.

I closed the door at the end of the hall after me and undressed as I left all of my clothes on the tiles then stood in the tub and drew the curtain. I turned the water on and it was cold to fill up the tub and I bent over and felt it between my fingers then stood up to hold my toes under the stream while I waited to switch up to the showerhead once it turned hot. The water was slow to drain as it had already started for my ankles and I bent over again to feel it in my hands, warmer but still not hot, but I pulled the tab anyway and switched it to the showerhead.

It was cold and I stood out of the way and waited a while before I came back under the stream as it warmed and it was good. It was dark with the curtain drawn and it was wet and warm, the steam rising against my skin and smoothing out the gooseflesh, but then the water turned too hot and burned my skin, so I stepped to the side again and I turned it back to cold, waiting a while as the steam went behind the curtain. I was cold standing there though, so I stepped into it again and feeling it against my chest I turned it hotter until it was as good as before.

I turned around and sank my head in the stream and waited for the water to get through all my hair until I could run my hands through it and let it fall past my shoulders as the pins and needles feeling came up my chest and back and met my shoulders in a hot flash that seared my skin from inside—shed the skin they say red the sin—but I shuddered it off and turned the water cold until it passed and I tried not to think of the fire in my stomach that needed to come out of me as soon as I stood in the wet warmth that wasn't unlike being in someone's mouth. I tried to remember all the blondes and brunettes and redheads I ever knew, but they were all the same to me.

They were the redhead I didn't know with the fire between their legs and mine in their mouth. I felt a hot flash coming and turned the water to cold and it left me with half a handful to start all over again—the venom of a snake they say the semen of a man—but what makes a man what he is but himself, everything larger the smaller one's hands are—three and four they say for and tree—the fingers and the palm tree in self-symmetry. The redhead and I breathed into each other then she covered her mouth and apologized for her bad breath from the drinking, how bad she felt but mine was worse and her breath didn't matter to me—flow snake flow they say snowflake snow—then there was all the goodness and all the badness that came together.

What was the difference between come and see and look and despair, if what goes down must come up in the end, but the circling down the drain, all of it spinning in circles the way we are all only ever spinning, down the drain in circles, but the water was slow to drain and it was all there in the tub still, which made me feel sick and I vomited with the morning sickness until there was nothing left in my body that wasn't up to my ankles. I picked up one foot then the other and some of the vomit stuck to each, but the water was warm enough on my shoulders for me to forget and to feel good.

You feel good, I always said when inside someone. You feel good.

I turned off the water and waited until most of it was done spinning down the drain, down the drain or dead in the trenches, what difference did it make, millions of millions of men led to their deaths, how many of them had died in my hands, the sons of my right hand. When the water had drained there was a red film left over most of the tub and I turned the faucet again and splashed a few handfuls across the tub to try to get rid of it, but when I couldn't I just turned the water up to the showerhead again and I kept it cold because I had heard the cold was good to tighten the skin on the body, but my skin would shed soon—itch they say scratch they say scratch they say itch—and my skin crawled again and tried to come off of me. I stood there withering with the cold on my chest, turning around for it to be against my back.

I turned the faucet to run the water from the showerhead to the tub when it was white enough again then I turned it off, but I stood in the cold water for a while before I pulled the curtain back and brushed some of the water off with my hands, wringing my hair as some strands stuck to my hands and I let them fall into the tub and got out to stand in the mirror, but it was steamed up and I could barely make out my figure as I started to dress.

I had to piss so I went over to the toilet and waited as the pain from the piss came in two fiery streams, one straight into the toilet water and one out along the rim to coat the tiles on the ground as I tried to redirect them both into the water, only to have the other stream rush into the water as the one went to the other side of the rim then over the edge, but when I was done I tore off some paper and dried the rim and I flushed the toilet and listened to the sound of the pipes rushing the water to fill the toilet again as the water spun down the drain.

I ate a handful of flowers on the way down to the train station, which it wasn't that bad to walk to in the morning, but my head rang in my ears and everything was red. I could still smell the vomit in my nose, though my breath was better with something in my stomach, pushing out to feel whatever was left that I hadn't thrown up yet then patting it down again as if I might keep the child. I didn't know what day it was passing one of the front yards where there was a little girl running naked in the grass and bursting bubbles her sister was blowing. I picked a flower I held onto for Eve and I stopped at a bodega to buy a bottle of sauvignon blanc because the two would go good together, the sauvignon blanc and a daffodil.

Down at the station I had the change left over from the bottle for a ticket and went through the turnstile then downstairs to where there were two tracks but no one waiting to go the other way. I straightened my sleeves to look more like all of the others waiting for the train into the city. They were all quiet and most of them read and most of them were women. The only times anyone read anymore were while waiting for the train to get there, but then again trains and time always went together. I read somewhere that women were the only ones who read.

The train came into the station, slowing down as several cars passed us until it came to a stop. The doors opened to let out no one, but I waited to let the others in before I did and none of them thanked me, so I went down a few rows to sit away from them and I sat next to a stained seat and cradled the bottle in my lap. It was a large one that looked like it was about a bottle and a half. It was much larger than what it was worth. I straightened my back against the chair and tried to fall asleep, turning my neck and resting my head against my shoulder, opening my eyes to look at the stain in the seat. I had once vomited on a seat next to me, maybe even the same seat.

When we came up above ground everyone sat starting straight ahead while the world went to the right—everyone is everything they say everyone is everyone else—and at the next stop there was a woman who sat across from me and looked like my mother before I was born. In the name of the mother the daughter and the holy host I crossed myself. The diamond on her ring rested up against her middle finger, so I tried not to look her in the eyes because God was in my eyes.

I transferred at the next station and watched as some of the others ran across the platform like the trains weren't timed together, all of them running just to sit down and wait until the train went underground and went west. There was no one on the train I wanted to look in the eyes. I wanted to drink from the bottle, but I didn't. I tried to fall asleep but couldn't keep my eyes closed.

There was an unattractive couple that looked happier than I ever would be, but I felt happy for them. There was a woman with a child who was crying. Life was learning to not cry all the time then learning to not mind children crying all the time. The woman looked good. I wanted to fuck her and be his father, but the only reason I would want to be a parent was to be a grandparent.

I got off at Embarcadero and went upstairs into a crowd of bums and commuters into the city, holding the bottle under my arm, not having to wait too long for a bus I got on and sat down near the front next to an old woman who looked like she would ride for a while. I came the same way before to the one side of Golden Gate Park when I was up the last time and went to see a redhead with a round face and reddened cheeks who looked good in profile but didn't as a portrait. I liked walking next to her and holding her hand, but I left her there without saying much after one night I was there with her and I never talked to her again and I couldn't remember her name.

I got off at Thirty-Fourth Avenue and walked down the

way I remembered where all the houses on the street looked like the same Victorian with bay windows, all a few stories and the same sorts of colors, most of them light pastels somewhere between tertiary and quaternary. Eve's looked like the others, walking up the half of a story of steps to the door, knocking and waiting a while then knocking again as she came to the door and she smiled. I always fell for someone the first time I saw them again.

Hey pretty pretty.

Hey yourself.

Hey.

How can you be dressed so nice, but look so bad.

I don't know, I looked down at myself then up at her. She was brown hair and a white-on-blue polka dot dress. You look nice too.

Aw shucks, you always know what to say right after I say it.

Aw shucks.

How are you, she asked and hugged me and she was soft.

Good, I said into her ear. Good.

Her hair smelled nice and she did too. I held onto her longer than she did me, but she laughed and I smiled. I smelled her hair again and said, You smell nice.

You smell like gasoline and cigarettes. That's dangerous.

Yeah, I should quit.

Well the two together.

It's odd cause I don't drive.

But you smoke.

Only when I'm drinking.

You're always drinking.

I'm not right now.

But you still smell like it.

That's just the cigarettes.

And the driving.

I felt her back and felt the buttons on the back of her dress and I asked her, How do you reach behind your back to button up your dress.

She pulled away and felt down my shirt and asked me, How do you button up your shirt.

What do you mean.

You misbuttoned it, she said and pulled my shirt out from my pants and redid the buttons. She stared up and down at me and brushed off my shoulders like they were covered in some dust and straightened my suit. She asked me, Where's your tie.

I don't know, I think I lost it.

She shook her head and said, I leave you alone for one year and this is what happens.

Well speaking of one year, I said and took the bottle out of its bag. This is for you.

You remembered.

What.

That I like to drink.

I laughed and said, Yeah let's drink to the first time we drank.

Well then, won't you come in.

Okay.

She closed the door behind me and pushed me forward and I could tell it was only girls living there. The hallway down to the rooms was mostly odds and ends showing how they were into art the same way all of the ones her age said they were, but still it looked good. She put her hands up on my shoulders and steered me into the kitchen.

I told her, I like what you've done with the place.

Well I knew you were coming, she said while she took the bottle from me.

Aw shucks.

She started to uncork the bottle and I tried to help, but she turned away from me and said no. I laughed and she opened it with a sound and started to drink straight from the bottle, but I stopped her and and said, Wait let me make sure it's not poisoned.

I took the bottle and drank.

Well.

Let me make sure. I drank again. Okay I don't think it's a slow act, I stopped and choked. I fell to the ground slow as I handed her the bottle and held my throat.

What is it.

I need some more to build up my tolerance, I said and reached for the bottle and she gave it to me and I drank. That's better, yeah. I stood up again.

I'm glad you'd die for me but I could use a drink, she said and she drank.

We could put it in the fridge for a while to get cold.

It's nice the way it is, she said and handed me back the bottle.

I eight you.

Do you really.

I do.

She smiled and said nothing.

Should we maybe get a good buzz going before we go cavorting, I asked but didn't bother to wait for what she said before I drank.

Yes. She scratched me at the start of my stomach. Buzz buzz buzz.

I laughed and pulled away from her, spilling some wine onto my chin then grabbing her wrist. She laughed and I bit into her and she made a *ch* sound through her teeth before going along with it, holding the back of her other hand to her forehead and looking away like she might faint.

Oh.

The wine was still on my tongue and I couldn't tell what she tasted like, but I let go, her wrist red from my teeth and I dried it off with my sleeve and I drank again.

Should we go somewhere then, I asked.

Yes. She took the bottle from me and drank. Do you wanna get high.

Sure. I took the bottle back and drank.

You don't have to if you don't want to.

I want to. Let's head out though too.

She led me through the opposite end of the kitchen and through a smaller room without much more than a couch and into another room where there was mostly clothes everywhere. She went through a bag left on her bed and I tried not to look around, but there were the same pictures and paintings and posters there always were. There were art supplies and old-fashioned cameras with their lenses and there were instruments out of their cases. I didn't say anything about any of them or the blouses and dresses and pants that had fallen off the clothes rack in the corner of the room, tossed and left where they were in another corner of the room. There were books standing up by themselves on a short dresser, but I didn't go over to look at them but watched her a while, going through her things as I stood over her shoulder and drank and waited.

What're you doing tomorrow, I asked. Do you wanna do something tomorrow.

Aren't we doing something today.

Today's good but I also wanna spend time with you tomorrow and I wanna make sure I get in early so you're not busy with something else tomorrow.

Okay, she said as she readied her bag but then stopped to hand me a bolo tie. Tomorrow it is.

So what do you wanna do today, I asked as I started to put it on before she helped me.

I don't know. I was waiting to do this with you tomorrow, but I guess we could do it today.

What is it.

Well, since it's the first nice day in a while, we should walk down to the beach.

We're here, she said. She pointed at a small star stickered onto the directory saying we were there then dragged her finger on and off some trails to where we were headed, a large green circle near the middle of the park. But we wanna go over here.

She leaned her head back against my shoulder and I stood behind her with my feet wide apart to make myself shorter, resting my jaw on her shoulder, holding onto the bottle in the bag for her in front of her stomach. I tried to make sense of what she said then handed her the bottle and she uncorked it to have some.

Is that where the buffalo roam.

She drank and it must have gone straight to her head as she nodded. I watched her drink again and I smiled to take back the bottle, which had become lighter since we had started. I drank some then she corked the bottle. She ran her finger over where we were going again.

I don't know how many of them there are but I've heard they're all supposed to be there, and it looks like that's what this says too, where the buffalo roam.

Okay good. I nodded then I turned her around to look at the windmill, which wasn't spinning, though it was still something to see, large and made of stone. I held her hand and I felt dumb, so I let go of her hand and I felt just as dumb. Shall we.

We had started walking to see where the buffalo roam because there was nothing else to do. It was too early in the day to keep up the kind of drinking we were doing, but it left us enough time to get just sober enough to enjoy the feeling of getting drunk all over again.

Let's go home, huh.

Yes, where the buffalo roam.

We walked on the small paved one-way road where there were no cars coming and held hands to not fall between drinking and to not fall behind. The road had split one way or another through the park and it didn't feel like we were going the right way, so we walked slowly and it wasn't too bad. She tied her hair back in one long brown ponytail that passed her shoulders. The sun was up in the sky, though I couldn't see much since it wasn't too bright with the trees as tall as they were and as many of them as there were there. We were heading either north or east through the park.

We gotta get off these main roads and see the country and such.

Yes I hear the country is lovely this time of day.

If you weren't so something, I wouldn't know what to say.

I feel like we're in some French film I like.

Is that right.

Oui.

Am I the bad boy, the wild child, the l'enfant terrible.

You're not as bad as you wish you were.

I laughed and told her, You're not so bad yourself.

We walked a while longer on the one-way road until we found the start of a dirt trail going the same way we were headed so we took it because we were getting close and it didn't matter which one we took since they ran alongside each other and we could still see the road.

Now I can show you how much of a frontiersman I am.

Is that right.

We have to think like a buffalo.

Do you feel at home where the buffalo roam.

I already feel like I'm thinking more like a buffalo.

Oh yeah, what would a buffalo think then.

I crouched down and circled around her almost on all fours with my hands up on my head like horns as she laughed and I circled around her again before I hugged her legs and felt her ass and bit her stomach.

She ran her fingers through my hair and said, You're thinking like a buffalo.

Yeah, I kissed her stomach and when I let go of her she took off with the bottle.

I ran after her and her ponytail bouncing back and forth, but she didn't run fast and I didn't run faster to catch her as the trail became less of one the farther I chased her. I couldn't tell how close the paved road was to us anymore and if everything was starting to wear off or if it was how long we had been walking together, but we ran and I could tell how there was nothing but us two. She stopped for no reason and I slowed down but still when I caught up to her came up behind her to put my arms around her and feel her ass against me as I smelled her hair and kissed her head.

What would a buffalo think we do next, she asked me between heavy breaths.

A buffalo would think we should drink.

You're very smart for a buffalo.

Thank you, you're very kind for a buffalo.

She uncorked and handed me the bottle in the brown bag. I got rid of the bag and drank then I handed the bottle back to her. We walked along the trail as it thinned and it wasn't bad feeling the way we were then. She walked ahead of me some but we walked side by side when we could and passed the bottle back and forth, though we had to give it up when the trail had thinned too much to let us walk together. The trees were closer together and we were covered in their shade.

Yes, they've definitely come through here, we'll have to track them, that's for sure, maybe we follow the buffalo, maybe turn around and head south for the winter.

She made a *ch* sound then asked me, Do you wanna hear a joke.

Okay.

What sort of celebration were all the buffalos waiting to go to.

I don't know.

The *bison*tennial.

I tried not to laugh, but she laughed at herself, which made me laugh.

She handed me the bottle and I drank enough to tell we were near the end of it, but I didn't say anything about that when I handed it back to her and she drank.

I don't know, I don't think, as good of a joke as it is, I mean it doesn't have much of a story.

There was a clearing just ahead of us that looked like it must have been what we were looking for right then. She handed me back the bottle corked and I held onto it while we walked.

Okay then tell me a story.

A story.

Yeah, a good story.

Okay, well.

We came into the clearing and we were in the sun and we went in through the thick grass that was all there was there, though around the edges there were tall trees, but there was nothing else there—Adam and Eve they say odd and even—and it was all green.

Well, once upon a time there was Eve.

We walked and with the sun up in the sky our shadows were under us and short.

And she was the protagonist of our story.

So far so good.

Why's that.

Things usually turn out well for the protagonist.

Oh.

At least better than for the contagonist.

Not always.

She dragged her feet through the grass and they made a rushing sound like we were on the beach and she was walking through the shallows. I listened to the sound her feet made while she dragged them and I didn't know what to say while we walked toward the middle of the clearing.

Have you heard this story before.

Yeah but I don't mind hearing it again.

Okay, so once upon a time there was Eve and she was such a liar.

She gasped and said, And here I thought she was the protagonist of our story.

She's more of a contagonist.

We slowed down some the closer we got to the middle and I got down on all fours and put my ear to the ground to try to hear the buffalo roam, but I couldn't make out anything but her feet on the grass while she circled around me.

Which sense do you think you could lose, she asked me.

I looked up at her and said, I don't know.

She took a red bandana from her bag and tied it tight around my eyes to spin me around a few times until she stopped and my head spun as I stuck my hands out to touch her chest but couldn't find her. I listened to her feet in the grass but then she stopped moving and I wanted to take it off and I told her, I don't think I could go without this one.

She laughed and I felt red and it was all I could see.

It's okay, she said as she came up to me and took off the bandana.

Which sense do you think you could lose.

She shrugged and I took the bandana from her and tied it around her eyes and spun her around then stopped and I laid her down and kissed her neck and she smiled then I kissed her breasts and belly button on the way down to kiss her down the front of her dress down to the bottom.

You don't have to do that.

I want to.

Someone'll see us.

I sat back on my legs and looked back and forth and said, There's no one else here.

She took the bandana off and sat up.

I eight you, I said.

I know.

Do you wanna give up looking for the buffalo.

I don't know.

I don't know where they are.

She shrugged.

I don't know where we are.

She redid herself as I stood up and drank then helped her up and her hands were as small as mine, but as we walked toward the other end of the clearing holding hands she took little steps to my steps. She let go of my hand and walked ahead of me and dragged her feet then stopped and I passed by her as she stared at me then I turned back and handed her the bottle.

And, she asked.

And.

Eve.

And Eve was lost.

Oh no. She drank some and wiped her mouth with the back of her hand.

And she was pretty pretty.

She made a *ch* sound again with her teeth together and her tongue up against them but her lips almost together.

She was pretty.

She smiled and looked away then back at me and dragging her feet slowly again like before as she came closer to me she pulled at the ends of the bolo tie she had given me to wear.

And she was very very pretty pretty.

I think you've had enough to drink.

I'll tell you when I haven't had enough.

Tell yourself.

She handed me the bottle and I lifted the bottle to my mouth. She started walking ahead of me again and I lifted the bottle higher until there was nothing left and she turned around and laughed at me, but I felt good and drunk and about as good as I had felt in the longest time. I walked after her and when I caught up to her I said, I think we're done with the drinking.

She stopped and made a face at me with her eyebrows together and her eyes squinted and she frowned to look like she was thinking hard. She asked me, When did we start drinking. Have we been drinking all of this time. When did we get to the end of the drinking.

I don't know, but I don't know what we're gonna bring to the big *bison*tennial now. I held the empty bottle up in the sun. Now this wasn't in bad taste was it, maybe we should get another one of these. Sauvignon blanc. I held the vowels and repeated them as we got to the end of the clearing. Sauvignon blanc.

Sauvignon blanc, she said with something of a hand gesture.

Sauvignon blanc.

Sauvignon blanc, she stretched it out.

When we reached the end of the clearing I turned around and threw the bottle as far as I could toward the middle then we walked for a while on another trail that didn't seem the right way until we came out the other side of the park and she asked me if I still wanted to get another sauvignon blanc because we were already so close to go to the beach.

When we got to the beach she said she didn't want to go to the sand yet but that we could go over to the cannon up on the hill looking over the beach, so we went toward the cannon instead as she walked ahead of me and it wasn't steep, but I put my hand against her back while we went up the sand covered path that was still sort of wet. There were vines with pink flowers all along it as we got to the top where there was the concrete enclosure for the cannon.

I think we just missed the demonstrations, she said reading a sign for the first of the month.

It's okay. I haven't known what day it is for several days now.

We went up to look at the cannon, which was covered in a puddled gray tarp, but I could tell it wasn't Spanish like all of the cannons at the presidio some miles from where we were. It was still something to look at though in its pit, surrounded by all sorts of pipes that would lift it above the battery when it was taken out for the demonstrations. Even when it wasn't ready to fire it was still always pointed at the sea.

We sat at the front of the concrete with our backs to the cannon and we looked over the beach and at the ocean too and the bridge some distance to the right, where we could see across the bay, farther to the left the ocean itself. I sat there breathing it in and the ocean smelled salty and good. We watched and we listened for the waves to turn white.

She was wearing large sunglasses that went back and forth between holding back her hair and holding down her nose and when she moved them down then and some of her brown hair was let down and she covered up her eyes and some of her freckles, she looked at me and smiled, which was all I could see of her.

I think I could sit here all day looking at the water, she said.

She sat back with her elbows on the concrete and stretched

her legs straight and watched several waves come in and out without saying anything, as though they wouldn't come in and out if she stopped watching them, as much as the cannon had been put there to keep it all where it was.

Me too, I said and I looked at her.

I've got such a good buzz buzz buzz going, she said.

What do you wanna talk about.

I don't know.

I think I could talk all day about eternity.

I think you think too much.

I don't think so.

We wrestled until her laughs sounded too labored and I sat up and she put her sunglasses back on and sat up next to me. I pulled her hands to me to see the few, thin blanched hairs on her arms in the sun and the shadows of her hands on me.

I like your hands, I said. Your hands are nice. I kissed them then let go of her and remembered the flower I had picked for her and I reached into my jacket pocket and gave her the daffodil.

What's all this then.

This is for you.

Oh. She held it up to her nose before she pushed her hair back and wore the flower behind her ear and showed off more of the freckles on her cheek and around her nose then pulled a strand of her thick brown hair above her lips and made a mustache for herself. Thank you sir.

You're welcome sir.

She let go of her hair and I kissed her and she said, Oh thank you sir.

You're welcome.

I kissed her again and longer and tongued her tongue too.

Well, she said. Thank you.

You don't have to thank me every time.

Okay, thanks.

I put my arm around her shoulder and she came in closer to me and she rested her head on my shoulder and I could hear her hair brushing up against my ear in the wind. I could hear the ocean through her hair and I kissed her head then rested mine on hers and we sat like that for a while.

Which eye do you look at when you look into someone's eyes, I asked as I looked at her.

I think I look back and forth at them both, she said as I watched her eyes go back and forth in mine then she smiled and pulled her glasses down.

The waves were breaking in white lines like cocaine. I sat up straight and I wasn't sure I could feel anything anymore. I turned to look at her and I pulled up her glasses to see if she was feeling the same. I squinted at her and she squinted at me, but everything must have worn off. I looked at the flower behind her ear then I went in to smell it or maybe to bite the head off, but I missed and I bit her ear instead and she smiled when I sat back.

I told her, I don't think I've ever been this sober.

How sober are you.

Not drunk.

Not drunk doesn't mean sober. She pawed at my stomach and asked me, Are you still buzzed.

No, I'm just not drunk. I'm sober.

Did you wanna go get another bottle.

No, I'm alright. I haven't eaten all day though.

Do you wanna get something to eat.

With you, I asked.

She sighed then asked, Why does everything have to be so hard with you.

Cause if it wasn't it'd be too easy.

Oh yeah.

Anything difficult is worth doing.

Well if nothing else, you are difficult.

So do you wanna get something to eat with me.

I thought you'd never ask, yes.

We kissed and both said thank you then went back to resting our heads against each others.

Tell me something, she said.

I eight you.

I eight you too.

I smiled and said nothing.

Tell me something else.

What about.

I don't know.

Do you wanna hear the rest of what happens to Eve.

I've already heard that one, but sure.

She sold seashells by the seashore, which is odd, you know, because who would even pay for seashells by the seashore. She was something though, because all the seashells are right there on the seashore.

Why was she selling seashells.

Well, she was waiting at the beach, watching the tide come in and out, waiting for when all of it would be hers.

All of what.

All of this, I said sweeping an open hand across the sea.

That's not how I remember the story going.

Yeah, I rewrote it some but it's all sort of the same.

But how does it all end.

Well the end is gonna cost you.

Oh yeah, she asked and kissed me.

Thank you, but that's not what I want.

What do you want.

I want you to want me.

Huh.

Then I'll tell you how it ends.

She laughed and said, Okay. You're wanted.

Aw shucks, thank you. But I'm wanted, I asked her. Are you gonna bring me in dead or alive.

She thought about it.

I asked her, How much is my head worth.

More than you think.

Okay.

So how does it end.

I don't know, but I think it needs a good end like a good bang.

We watched the waves come in and out and I looked at her once or twice but couldn't tell how long we had been sitting there since we hadn't said anything, but then she reached into her pocket and pulled out her hand, index and middle fingers together pointed at me, other two fingers pointed at herself. I held my hands up as she pulled back her thumb then bent it forward.

Bang, she said. Bang.

I fell over dead as she stood up and took off while I sat there lifeless for a while before I stood up too and saw her running down to the beach. I ran after her, wondering whether we might have stayed where we were all day if I hadn't died. I followed her down to the sand and where she had taken her shoes and socks off, standing there to do the same and to leave everything behind there to go after her on the beach. I fell in the sand and crawled on all fours until I got up again and started running to catch her, though I didn't know why or what I would do if I caught her, but she slowed down in the low tide and all I did was follow her as she dragged her feet in the wet sand.

We would fall down in the shallows and listen to the ocean wave at us—shush they say shush—and wake us not to wonder whether we were the lost ones or were not.

DRDOCTORDRDOCTOR.COM

dD